Inside illustrations by Raymond Abel

SCHOLASTIC INC.
New York Toronto London Auckland Sydney

ISBN 0-590-40397-4

 Published by Scholastic Inc., 730 Broadway, New York, NY 10003, by arrangement with J.B. Lippincott, a division of Harper & Row Publishers, Inc.

12 11 10 9 8 7 6 5 4 3 2 1 11 6 7 8 9/8 0 1/9

Printed in the U.S.A. 11

Contents

The Lonely Island

IT WAS a shining, golden afternoon in early November. The grass on Nine-Mile Marsh had turned a dark burnt-orange color and the water in the creeks glistened like blue enamel.

Lucille Pierce loved the way her bicycle seemed to fly over the level marsh road as she pedaled home from school. The school bus swished past her before she had gone very far. It looked like a fat yellow pumpkin rolling along. The children waved and shouted from its windows, delighted to be winning in the race toward home.

When the bus was out of sight the loneliness of the marsh and the chill of the fall afternoon settled heavily on Lucille's spirits. It didn't even help to remember it was Friday. What was there to do on the weekend when there was no one to play with? Kevin and Brent would be around, of course, but they didn't care about having a girl tagging along with them.

The Saturday Club was to blame. Some of the girls in her class had started it, and Pam and Linda, the only girls of her own age who lived at Pinewood Acres, belonged. Now they stuck together all the time and went off to their stupid club meetings on Saturdays. Lucille told herself scornfully that she wouldn't *want* to join the club, but it hurt not to have been asked.

Pinewood Acres was a housing development at the northern end of the marsh. Miles of watery grass and salt creeks stretched down the Maine coast from there all the way to Old Orchard Beach. It was a wide, empty region that seemed to belong to the seabirds — the gulls and herons and geese — whose wild cries deepened its loneliness.

Lucille heard a shout and turned to look behind her. Kevin MacIntosh was pedaling furiously along, trying to catch up. His cheeks were red and he was puffing as he pulled his new Sting Ray bike up beside her old one. Kevin was on the plump side and he got out of breath easily.

"I thought you and Brent took the bus," Lucille said.

"Well, now you know what *thought* did." Kevin's voice was surprisingly sharp.

Lucille stared at him. "What's the matter?"

"Your brother's mad. We had a spelling match and — "

"*Oh* — oh, I can guess what happened. You were captain and you didn't choose him."

"I did too choose him," Kevin sputtered. "I chose him the very first, even though he can hardly spell *cat* right. My side lost, too."

"Well gee, I don't see why he's mad, then. I wouldn't choose Brent. Daddy says he's a natural-born poor speller."

"He's a natural-born *nut,*" Kevin declared. "You know how he does — holds his head up and speaks loud and fast without taking time to think. *Personal* was his word, and he spelled it p-e-r-c-i-n-a-l — "

"And you laughed," Lucille accused him. "That's what he's mad about."

"Everybody laughed. We couldn't help it. It was funny." Even now an unwilling smile made Kevin's lips twitch.

"But you know Brent hates to be laughed at. He'll be mad at you all weekend. It's too bad."

Kevin nodded unhappily. "Darn it all, I had something special I wanted him to do this afternoon, too."

Lucille couldn't help giggling at the dark frown on his face. "What was it?" she asked.

He pointed toward an island in the marsh not far ahead of them. "I want to go over there. This might be the last chance we'd ever have to explore around those old buildings. The new owner is coming on Monday."

"Explore Moody's Island!" Lucille sounded shocked. "Gee, would you dare?"

The island was a low knoll in the marsh with a few oak trees and an old, weather-beaten farmhouse on it. Several other dilapidated buildings were partly hidden under the trees. A narrow lane ran out to the island from the marsh road.

"I think Mrs. Moody must have been a hermit — if you could call a woman a hermit," Kevin said. "She lived alone and never had visitors or went anywhere. That's being a hermit, isn't it? I'd like to see what her house is like, close to."

"You can see what it's like from here. You aren't supposed to go over to it. It's private property."

"There's nobody around to see. Miss Rand's coffee shop is the only place nearby, and there aren't any customers at this time of day." Kevin's blue eyes sparkled excitedly. "Hey, will you go with me?"

Lucille hesitated. The thought of going over to the island was exciting, but it was scary, too. Had Kevin forgotten about the Moody noises? Everybody knew the strange, wailing sounds that came from the island when a storm wind blew in from the sea. Lucille had heard them herself.

"What about the noises?" she asked.

"My father says it must be the wind blowing into a chimney or catching under the eaves of the old house that makes those queer sounds," Kevin told her. "He says it's silly to think they have anything to do with old John Moody and his boat being lost at sea long ago. There's nothing to be scared of."

"I guess nobody really believes it's John Moody's ghost who makes them," Lucille admitted, "but they scare me just the same."

"Well, I'm not scared. I'm interested in hermits, that's why I want to go over there. I've been reading a book about an old hermit who hid his money all over his house, even in the woodshed and in his dog's kennel. People found it in all kinds of crazy places after he was gone."

Lucille laughed. "We won't find any money on the island. Mrs. Moody was poor."

Kevin knew from her words that she was going with him. "We'll have to hurry," he said. "It gets dark by half past four, these days."

They flew past the island lane and The Blue Goose, Miss Rand's coffee shop. They had to go home and change into their old clothes before they could go exploring.

"I hope I don't have to take care of Debbie or anything," Lucille said, as they approached their own houses. "And what if Brent wants to come with us?"

"Let him come. *I'm* not mad. I'll meet you in fifteen minutes."

Lucille found her brother in the kitchen eating a

sandwich and drinking Moxie which he kept in the refrigerator all the time just for himself. Mrs. Pierce was making a sandwich for Lucille, and Debbie, the baby of the family, was contentedly painting in her coloring book.

"Mamma, can I go bike riding with Kevin?" Lucille asked. "It's nice out this afternoon."

"But you've just ridden all the way home from school," her mother protested. "I shouldn't think you'd feel like any more of it right now. Is Brent going too?"

Brent spoke up loudly. "I'm playing football over on the lot with Jim and Larry." He put his Moxie bottle back in the refrigerator and went off to his room to change his clothes.

"He's mad at Kevin," Lucille said. She explained about the spelling match while she ate her sandwich and drank a glass of milk. Mamma laughed softly, but said with a shake of her head, "Poor Brent. He'll be miserable until he makes up with Kevin. I *do* wish he wasn't so quick to get angry."

Lucille put on her warm corduroy slacks and jacket and tied a blue wool ear-warmer over her light hair. She was just stepping out the door when Kevin arrived. He saw Brent running across the lots to Jim Dalesandro's house and his blue eyes looked disappointed.

They rode swiftly away from the crowded development onto the marsh road. There were a few farms on the outskirts of Pinewood Acres. One of these was the Turner farm, a bleak gray house surrounded by acres of cabbage gardens. Kevin and Lucille kept their eyes straight ahead as they passed it. They didn't want to see Pedro, or hear his pleading cries for attention.

Pedro was a small, patient, gray donkey. Mr. Turner had taken him in one of the endless "trades" he was always making. He had expected to sell him again quickly, but nobody seemed to want a donkey. So, for a long time now, the poor animal had been neglected and almost forgotten. Mr. Turner staked him out in the fields while he waited for a chance to trade him to someone else.

Lucille always felt sad when she saw Pedro tied in the muddy garden with hardly anything to graze on and no chance to move around. She stopped to pet him whenever she was sure neither Mr. Turner nor his son George would see her.

"I wouldn't want George Turner to catch us riding out to Moody's Island," she said, glancing nervously back over her shoulder.

Kevin was gazing straight ahead. "There aren't any cars at The Blue Goose," he observed. "Miss Rand must be getting things ready for supper. She won't notice us."

They turned their bicycles into the island lane just as the sun dropped behind a low bank of clouds. The water in the creek looked suddenly black and the air was cold. Beyond the bare trees on the island the buildings loomed up, bleak and forbidding. Lucille felt like turning back, but Kevin hopped quickly off his bike and led the way to the house. The shades were drawn behind all the windows, so they couldn't see inside.

"Let's go around back," he suggested.

Lucille trailed timidly behind him. She glanced at the tumbledown sheds and noticed in surprise that the big door of the barn was partly open. She hoped Kevin wouldn't want to go in there. It would be dark as midnight inside.

"Why don't we go up on the knoll and look around?" she asked, pointing to the rising ground behind the house.

"Okay," he agreed.

The knoll wasn't very high. Its outer edge dropped straight down to the creek which swirled close to the island there. From the top, the children could see across the marsh to the sand dunes of Outer Beach. Gulls flew over their heads, uttering strange, loud cries as they headed toward the open sea.

"Mrs. Moody was a hermit, all right," Kevin observed with satisfaction. "She never would have stayed on this lonely island all by herself if she hadn't been."

Lucille stopped to pick up a creamy yellow stone from the path. She rubbed her fingers over it and then, reluctantly, dropped it. "It's not quite smooth enough," she sighed.

"You and your feeling stones," Kevin scoffed.

"I like them. Rubbing one in your hand is as good as chewing gum if you happen to feel nervous. And I happen to feel nervous right now."

Kevin turned to run down the slope. "Let's take a look in the barn," he called.

"No! It's too dark in there!"

"Aw, come on. Don't be chicken — just because you're a girl."

Lucille didn't want to be left alone in the gloomy yard. She followed as far as the barn door and peered inside. "I'll wait for you here," she said. She kept her feet poised to run if she should need to.

Kevin took a few cautious steps, then stopped to listen. "Hey — do you hear something?" he whispered.

A heavy plank in the loft above their heads creaked faintly. The creak was followed by the sound of someone treading over the floor.

"I hear it all right!" Lucille gasped. "Let's go!"

Kevin slid through the door's opening and the two of them ran wildly across the yard to the spot where they had left their bicycles.

The Problem of Pedro

LUCILLE was so nervous she dropped her bicycle twice before she managed to climb onto it. She and Kevin pedaled swiftly up the lane. "Gee, I was scared!" she exclaimed, glancing back over her shoulder. "I wonder who that was — in the barn?"

"We ought to stick around and find out," Kevin answered. "Probably it was only Clyde Moody. We don't need to be scared of *him.*"

Lucille frowned thoughtfully. She knew Clyde was the only member of the Moody family who was still living. Old John Moody had been his uncle. But Clyde didn't have any right to be on the island now. It belonged to somebody else. She looked around for a place where she and Kevin might hide while they waited for Clyde to come along. On each side of the lane there was nothing but tall grass and cat-o'-nine-tails. They couldn't duck down in them because water sucked around the roots. The tide was still quite high.

"Couldn't we hide around the corner of The Blue Goose?" she asked.

Kevin shook his head. "Miss Rand might see us." He rummaged in his pockets and pulled out some change. "Seven, eight — eleven cents. Oh heck, that isn't enough to get each of us a soda."

"I don't want any," Lucille said. "You get one. We'll sit by the front windows and watch the island while you drink it. We've *got* to find out who was up in that barn loft. Come on!"

They crossed the road and parked their bicycles in the yard of the white coffee shop. The lights were on inside, shining cheerfully through the many-paned windows.

Miss Rand was surprised to see them. She opened a bottle of root beer for Kevin with a shiver. "Brr! It's a cold night for an ice cold drink. I'd lots rather pour a cup of tea for you."

Kevin pretended to shiver, too. "Brrr — tea!" he said with a grin.

Instead of sitting down at the counter as Miss Rand expected them to do, the children went over to a table near the front window. Kevin sipped his drink slowly to make it last as long as possible and he and Lucille peered out into the blue dusk. From this brightly

lighted room it was hard to see anything in the lane leading to the island.

"Isn't it kind of late and dark for you kids to be bicycling over the marsh?" Miss Rand asked.

"We've been over to Moody's Island," Kevin told her boldly. "We wanted to explore it before the new owner got there."

Miss Rand set down the kettle of hot water she was holding and stared at them in surprise. "Weren't you scared? I suppose you were hoping to see the ghost who makes the Moody noises."

Lucille shook her head. "We know there isn't any ghost. We just thought it would be exciting to see the old house and everything, close to, while we had the chance."

Miss Rand's face grew serious. "I can't understand why Margaret Moody left that island to a perfect stranger. People say she had never even met Arnold Lindsay — whoever he is. She never even saw him. She couldn't have, because she never saw anybody except her doctor or her lawyer or the boy who brought her groceries."

Kevin nodded wisely. "She was a hermit all right. That was why I wanted to see what her house was like."

"Have other people been going over there since Mrs. Moody died?" Lucille asked.

Miss Rand went back to filling her coffee-maker. "Nobody goes there. You couldn't hire them to."

Lucille thought of the footsteps in the barn loft and raised her eyebrow significantly. "*Somebody* does," she whispered to Kevin.

Then her eyes met Miss Rand's sharp glance in the mirror behind the counter and she wondered uneasily if she had been overheard.

"I'm sorry for Clyde Moody," Miss Rand went on. "Mrs. Moody's husband, John, was Clyde's uncle, you know. Clyde is the only one left of the Moody family. Mrs. Moody should have left the island to him." She shook her head, sputtering, "Arnold Lindsay — a man she never even *met*."

"But Clyde Moody isn't much good, is he?" Kevin asked. "I mean, people say he drinks all the time and he never keeps a job — "

"He might straighten out if he had the family property. It might give him some self-respect." Miss Rand tossed her head and added crossly, "I hadn't any patience with old Mrs. Moody. I tried to be neighborly when I bought this shop. I went to her house three times, but she wouldn't even answer my knock on the door."

It was clear from her indignant tone of voice that Miss Rand's feelings had been hurt. You could hardly blame her, Lucille thought, for not approving of Mrs. Moody.

Lucille's eyes strayed from the window to the blue-painted tables and colorful walls of the coffee shop. Miss Rand was such a solid, sensible-looking woman she seemed to be all business. Yet the shop walls were hung with the loveliest pictures Lucille had ever seen. Miss Rand collected them and loved them. Some were copies of famous masterpieces, and some were oil paintings of the marshes and the sea done by people who lived nearby. They were all beautiful, she thought, as she turned back to the window.

"Are you children watching for someone?" Miss Rand asked after a while.

Kevin drew in the last drops of his soda with a loud gurgle.

"We're just looking at the island," Lucille explained. "It sure is lonely at this hour of day. I wonder if the Moody noises will stop when someone new is living there?"

"I hope not," Miss Rand said quickly. "The Moody noises are good for my business. People often come here in bad weather because they hope to hear them. They like to think the strange noises have something to do with old John Moody's having been lost in that northeast storm. You've heard them yourselves, haven't you?"

Some customers came in just then, so the children didn't try to answer.

"We'll have to go home," Kevin said. "It's really getting dark now."

They pushed their chairs back and hurried to the door. As soon as they got used to the dimness outside they realized it wasn't as dark as it had seemed when they were looking from the window of the coffee shop.

Lucille stopped before they had gone very far and pointed toward the marsh. "Hey, there's a boat over there near the island!"

Kevin stared. He could barely make out the rowboat that was disappearing in the shadows of the tall cat-o'-nine-tails.

"So *that's* how he gets to the island without being seen!" he muttered thoughtfully. "I bet it is Clyde Moody. He's a fisherman and he's always fooling around in boats."

It was terribly unsatisfying to stumble into such a mysterious situation without being able to do more than guess at what it was all about. Lucille said gloomily, "We'll probably never know who it was."

As they approached the Turner farm the smell of freshly cut cabbages hung heavy on the air. It drove away the clean tang of the marsh and the sea. From one of the cutover gardens behind the house a loud hiccuping sound reached the children's ears.

"Uh-hee, uh-hee, uh-hee — "

They stopped a moment to listen.

"Uh-hee — *Haw!*" the little donkey finally managed to bray. He was excited to know his friends were near.

They laid their bikes on the grass and ran across the cabbage garden to where they saw the big-eared, knobby-kneed animal straining at the end of his rope.

"What a place to leave him!" Kevin scolded.

"There isn't anything but old cabbage roots for him to eat. I bet they'll leave the poor thing out here all night, too."

Lucille leaned her blond head against the donkey's neck. "Poor baby," she whispered. "Poor, lonely baby."

Pedro rubbed his rough ears on her cheek. Then he snuffled at her hands as if he hoped to find something good to eat.

"His feet are worse than ever," Kevin observed, bending down to examine them. The hoofs were so overgrown Pedro could hardly stand on them. They should have been cut and trimmed, but they had been let grow until they were as large as a pair of Dutch wooden shoes. The little animal had to stand with his legs spread out and his weight resting on his bent ankles. "Nobody takes care of him at all."

"He's hungry, too," Lucille said.

"If we only lived on a farm I'd get Daddy to buy him for me," Kevin sighed. "But we haven't any place to keep him. I'm coming back to bring him some food tonight, though. I can do that much."

As they tore themselves away and picked up their bicycles, Lucille said firmly, "We've got to find a way to help him. We've *got* to."

They were so angry about Pedro's plight they almost forgot about Moody's Island. Kevin's indignation made him pedal his Sting Ray so fast Lucille couldn't keep up with him. As she pushed her bike along she told herself hopefully that she and Kevin — and Brent, too — could surely find a way to save Pedro before his feet got so bad he was really crippled. There must be *somebody* who would like to have such a nice, patient little animal.

"Helping him is more important than finding out who was in Mrs. Moody's barn," she said to Kevin. "We ought to try. We ought to *really* try."

The New Owner

AFTER HER RIDE across the marshes Lucille was happy to step into the warm kitchen at home and smell clam chowder simmering on the stove.

"*And* mince pie," Brent said, wrinkling his nose as he sat down to the table with his family.

Lucille ate two bowlfuls of chowder. Then she laid her spoon down and sighed. "Gee, I wish that poor little donkey at Turner's could have a good meal like this."

"Do donkeys like clam chowder?" Debbie asked wonderingly.

Brent and Daddy burst out laughing, and Lucille explained that she hadn't meant she wished Pedro could have chowder. "I just wish he could have a good full meal."

"I think I'll ride over there and take him some food," Brent said. "I bet the Turners leave him out all night."

Lucille started to say "Kevin is going to — " but she stopped. It might be better not to mention Kevin's plan to feed Pedro. If he and Brent should meet over there, they might forget their quarrel and be friends again. She told about going to Moody's Island with Kevin, instead.

"It probably *was* Clyde Moody who was prowling around the barn loft," her father said. "He's pretty sore about not getting the family property. There may be things that belonged to his uncle that he intends to take before anyone can stop him."

Mamma looked at him questioningly. "I should think that letters and family pictures and things would be in the house rather than the barn."

"Clyde might have been hunting for tools or fishing gear," Daddy answered. "You could hardly blame him for going over the whole place while he was at it."

"Miss Rand can't understand why old Mrs. Moody left the island to a man she never even met," Lucille told them.

Her mother shook her head. "Everybody in town is wondering about it. If the old lady didn't like Clyde and didn't want him to have the property, why didn't she leave it to her doctor, or her lawyer, or even Miss Rand — someone she at least *knew*?"

"If she never met this Arnold Lindsay how did she know his name?" Brent asked. "Did she just pick it out of a telephone book?"

Daddy shrugged his shoulders. "Maybe she read something about him in the newspaper. He could be a writer or an artist or even a movie star, for all we know."

"Arnold Lindsay," Lucille murmured. "Gee, that does sound like a movie star's name! I wonder if he is one?"

"Mrs. Moody wouldn't know any movie stars. She didn't even have a TV," Brent scoffed.

"The man is going to run into trouble as soon as he gets here," Daddy said. "Clyde Moody has hired a lawyer to try to break the will. He is going to try to prove that the old lady wasn't in her right mind when she left everything to a perfect stranger."

Mamma and Daddy went on discussing the question of the will while they ate their dessert, but Lucille hardly listened. She was lost in a daydream of a handsome young movie star named Arnold Lindsay who was coming to live on the island.

Brent pushed back his chair. "Can I take these biscuits to Pedro?" he asked. "There are only three left."

Mamma nodded. "And give him the rest of the box of cornflakes on the pantry shelf. It's getting stale."

Lucille was so tired from all the riding she had done that afternoon she was glad to settle down on the couch in the den with her newest library book. Her mind was partly on the story and partly on Kevin and Brent. Would they reach the Turner farm at the same time, or would they miss each other?

Just as the clock was striking seven the two boys came bustling into the house. They had met in the windy darkness of the cabbage field and had fed Pedro and ridden home together as if they had never quarreled.

"I guess you got your wish, Lucille," Brent told her. "Pedro had a full meal and *then* some."

He and Kevin giggled and clattered up the stairs to play with the set of racing cars Brent had got for his birthday.

"We're going to feed him every night, after dark, when George Turner can't see us," Brent called down over his shoulder.

Lucille felt almost sorry the boys were friends again. Now they would be together every minute. She would have to push herself into their company if she wanted any more adventures on Nine-Mile Marsh. When Brent and Kevin were on good terms they forgot anyone else existed.

She thought of the two free days ahead of her, and sighed. Darn that old Saturday Club anyway! It had spoiled all her fun. She couldn't help wondering why she hadn't been invited to belong to it. Why would they ask Pam and Linda to join and leave her out?

She tried to think of something she could do that would show those club members she had just as much fun as they did — and more. But she needed a friend for that.

There was a new girl, Barbara Rosen, who had moved into the big house at the end of the street. She didn't belong to the Saturday Club, and she didn't seem to care. The only trouble was, she *liked* to stay by herself. She didn't seem to want to be friends with anyone.

"I'll just have to tag along with the boys whether they want me or not," Lucille sighed in discouragement.

The weekend turned out to be mild and cloudy, with fog hanging over Nine-Mile. The children rode their bicycles back and forth past the island, gazing curiously at it each time they went by. The bare trees and dark roofs of the buildings looked as if they stood on the edge of nowhere, with the fog blotting out the marsh behind them.

The radio weatherman predicted a storm, and he was right. By Monday morning a northeaster began to howl across the marshes. It lasted all day Tuesday, too. Wednesday was so dark and cold that the last sprinkles of rain turned to a flurry of snowflakes in the afternoon.

Lucille worried about Pedro during the long spell of bad weather. She made up her mind to go and see him as soon as she got home from school that afternoon, snow or no snow.

"We've got to take him some food," she insisted to the boys, as they left the bus at their corner.

Kevin looked up at the threatening sky. "It's awfully cold."

"I just hope George Turner won't be around," Brent said. "He gets mad if he sees anybody trying to help the poor donkey."

"I bet Pedro has been missing us," Kevin mused. "George never knew about all the food we took to him on the weekend nights."

Brent thought it might be better to wait until after dark this time, too, but Lucille insisted they should go right away. "They might put him in the barn for good, now that the weather has turned so cold," she said. "Then we couldn't feed him at all."

They collected some cookies and bread, and Brent added a tomato. "Billy Jones's horse loves tomatoes, and maybe Pedro will, too."

When they set out, Lucille's thoughts turned to the problem of finding a new home for the donkey. The only person she could think of who might help was Sam Estabrook, the contractor who had built the houses on Pinewood Acres. He was a friendly, jolly sort of person, and he lived next door to Kevin. He might know somebody who could give the donkey a home.

"You live near Mr. Estabrook, Kevin," she said, as they drew close to the Turner farm. "Couldn't you ask him to help us find a home for Pedro? He helped you boys when you wanted a place to play football. He let you use that vacant lot."

Kevin shook his head. "He wouldn't do anything about this. He and the Turners are friends."

"Mr. Estabrook only helped us with the football field because Pinewood Acres is his property and he wants people to hear what a great place it is," Brent declared. "He's not so bighearted and friendly as you might think."

Glancing ahead, the children saw Mr. Turner and George working in their yard. They rode by as fast as they could, hoping the two men would be too busy to notice them.

"Hey, look! There's somebody over there with Pedro!" Brent exclaimed, as they approached the cabbage field beyond the house.

They slowed down and gazed curiously at the stranger who was patting the little donkey. He was a small man with a bald head and a nose that was reddened from the cold wind. He bent down to look at Pedro's overgrown hoofs just as the children hopped off their bicycles and hurried toward him. When he glanced up, Lucille was surprised to see how bright and piercing his blue eyes were, behind his glasses.

"Is this your donkey?" he asked in a sharp tone.

All three children shook their heads. The long tassel on Lucille's wool cap shook wildly and so did her light hair that hung down beneath it.

"He belongs to the Turners," Kevin said, nodding

toward the gray house.

"Well, it's a crime for an animal to be left with his hoofs so overgrown he can't stand on them. Tied out on a bitter day like this, too! The rope is so short he can't run around enough to get warm, and *I* think he's hungry." The stranger's voice was loud and accusing as if he still thought the children must be to blame for Pedro's condition.

Lucille glanced nervously toward the house. She wished he would speak more softly so the Turners wouldn't hear him.

"We came to feed him," Kevin said.

"And I brought him a tomato," Brent added, pulling it out of his pocket. He held it out to the donkey, who snuffled it into his big mouth eagerly.

"Now *that* was a good idea," the stranger said in a friendlier tone. "The poor animal needed something like that."

He continued to talk in his loud, firm voice while he squatted down and took one of Pedro's big hoofs in his hands. "Sheer cruelty! How can the people of this community permit an animal to be kept in such miserable condition?"

A deep voice from just behind Lucille's shoulder broke in angrily, "Leave that donkey be! His condition is none of your business."

It was Mr. Turner. He and George had heard the stranger's voice and had come to see what was going on.

"You'd better get off our property," George added, jerking his head toward the road. "*All* of you."

Lucille was frightened. Mr. Turner looked angry enough to start a fight with the little man who was trying to help Pedro.

The stranger looked him in the eye and asked consideringly, "How much will you take for him?"

Mr. Turner hesitated. It was easy to see that he didn't want to have any dealings with the man who had spoken so insultingly about Pedro's condition. At the same time, he hated to pass up a chance to sell the donkey.

"Sixty dollars," he muttered at last. "And that's dirt cheap for a two-year-old, good-tempered animal. He's a real Mexican burro."

Lucille held her breath. Would the odd little man pay that much? Oh, if only he would! If only Pedro could have a good home at last!

The man took out his wallet. "I'll give you twenty-five," he said curtly. He held out the bills. "That's all I've got."

Mr. Turner's mouth tightened in disgust. "Twenty-five dollars! Are you crazy? I traded three truck loads of firewood for him only last year. You can keep your twenty-five dollars, and clear out of here."

The children gasped at his furious tone of voice, and stepped back toward the fence.

The stranger's blue gaze grew hard. He continued to hold out the money. "Would you prefer to discuss this with the S.P.C.A.?" he asked in a steely voice. "I could have someone here before night to examine the donkey's hoofs and general condition. You'd find a court case would cost you more than you'd lose by selling him to me."

George Turner stepped forward. "Why you — "

Mr. Turner shook his head at his son. He reached out and snatched the money from the stranger's hand. "Take him — it'll be good riddance. Save me the cost of feeding him all winter." He added sneeringly, "I don't know how you think you're going to get him home with you, but that's *your* problem."

He strode off toward his house. George started to follow but turned to say to the wide-eyed children, "You better get out of here and *stay* out."

The stranger patted Pedro's head and sighed. "There goes the last of my ready cash. I haven't got a bit of use for this animal, either. How I'm going to get him home, with those clumsy feet of his, I don't know." His blue eyes moved from Lucille's face to Kevin's. "I don't suppose you children could take him?"

"We'd love to," Lucille said, "but we haven't any room. We live over there in the development — Pinewood Acres."

Brent exclaimed, "Gee, you were great, the way

you stood up to Mr. Turner!" and Kevin added admiringly, "Yeah, you sure told him off!"

"There's a farm about a mile from here where they have a truck," Lucille said. "We could ride over and see if they would come and move Pedro for you. Where do you live?"

The little man blew his nose and considered the problem for a moment. Then he stuffed his handkerchief back into his pocket and said decisively, "Thank you for the suggestion, but I guess the donkey will be able to make it as far as my house. I'll go slowly and let him walk in the grass at the edge of the road. I'm Arnold Lindsay and I live on Moody's Island."

"You are!"

"You do!"

The boys were dumbfounded.

"Arnold *Lindsay?*" Lucille repeated incredulously. She thought of all the things Daddy had said the new owner of the island might be — a writer, an artist, even a movie star. And all he was was this nice, harmless, kindly little man with a bald head and a slightly dripping nose!

A Blue Linen Handkerchief

"I'M GOING to look pretty funny, plodding down the road with this animal," Mr. Lindsay said, as he untied Pedro's rope.

"I'll lead him for you," Kevin offered good-naturedly. "I'd be glad to."

"We'll all help. We can leave our bikes right here. Mr. Turner doesn't own the roadside." Lucille's voice was firm. She took the rope out of Mr. Lindsay's hand before he realized what she was doing. With one arm around Pedro's neck she began to lead him out of the cabbage field.

The little group made slow progress through the cold, darkening afternoon. Pedro stumbled over his own clumsy hoofs and stopped now and then to look questioningly at the children.

"I'll have to have a veterinary come and clip those hoofs, the very first thing," Mr. Lindsay said. "Is there a vet in town?"

"There's Dr. Phillips," Lucille told him.

"I suppose I could telephone to him from The Blue Goose, couldn't I? The phone in my house has been disconnected." He added with a smile, "By the way, I don't know your names, yet."

They had plenty of time to get acquainted on the long walk to the island. Kevin told Mr. Lindsay how curious people were about him. "They can't understand how Mrs. Moody came to leave everything to you when she didn't even know you, you see."

Mr. Lindsay blew his reddened nose again, and shook his head. "I can't understand it either. I never heard of *her* until I received her lawyer's letter telling me she had left all her property to me. It was like a gift from heaven. I needed a place that would be quiet and peaceful enough so I could do some writing."

"Oh — you're an author!" Lucille exclaimed. "Mrs. Moody must have read some of your books. That must be how she knew you."

The little man smiled. "You couldn't possibly call me an author — at least, not yet. All I've ever written is a few articles for the newspapers. But maybe that was how Mrs. Moody knew of me, at that."

"She read a lot," Kevin told him. "Her mailbox used

to be so stuffed with papers and magazines the mailman couldn't close it half the time."

Mr. Lindsay's face looked pleased. "I'd be happy to think she liked my articles all that much. By the way, can you children tell me anything about the weird noises I heard during yesterday's storm? Is it always like that on the marshes?"

Brent told him about the Moody noises. "Some people think they are kind of ghostly, on account of old Mr. Moody and his fishing boat being lost off Outer Beach years ago in a northeast storm. It's only when that kind of a storm is blowing up that the noises are heard."

Mr. Lindsay's eyes twinkled. "But *you* don't think it's a ghost who makes them?"

"Heck, no," Brent declared. "But I'd like to know what *does*."

"Could it be a foghorn somewhere down the coast or out on an island at sea?" Kevin asked.

"It's not that far away. It sounded as if it were right under my feet in the old house. I went down cellar to see, in fact, but there was nothing there. You children will have to come over, during the next northeaster, and see what *you* think."

The boys exchanged pleased smiles and Lucille gave a little skip of happiness. It would be fun to explore the house and island, and to play with Pedro when he was well cared for.

"You can learn to ride the donkey as soon as his feet

are fixed up," their new friend added, almost as if he had been reading Lucille's mind. "The exercise would be good for him. I'd hardly dare ride him around the place myself. People would certainly think I was an odd stick, if I did."

He *was* a little bit odd, Lucille admitted to herself frankly. But he was nice.

She was surprised to see, as they came within sight of The Blue Goose, that the coffee shop was dark. Ordinarily lights would be twinkling behind the windowpanes on a gloomy afternoon like this.

When she looked beyond the shop toward the island she was even more surprised to see someone who looked like Miss Rand hurrying up the lane to the road. The woman turned in the opposite direction and walked rapidly away, as if she were hoping not to be seen. If it was Miss Rand, and if she had been over to the island to make a call, why didn't she come and tell Mr. Lindsay so? She disappeared around a curve in the road. Mr. Lindsay and the boys were talking together about getting a saddle for Pedro and didn't seem to have noticed.

It was hard for Pedro to walk in the rutted lane, and even harder to persuade him to step on the rattling planks of the bridge over the creek. When they were finally across, Mr. Lindsay said he could manage the rest of the way if the children thought they should go home. "It's getting late," he reminded them.

"We don't care," Kevin replied. "We want to help you get Pedro into the barn."

Lucille was as eager as the boys were to see the donkey safely settled for the night. They could run all the way back to the Turner farm where they had left their bikes, if they had to in order to get home by suppertime.

"It's awfully lonely here," Brent observed.

Mr. Lindsay drew a deep breath. "I like it," he said, glancing off across the marsh toward the sea.

He rolled the big barn door wide open to let in as much light as possible. There were two stalls that had been used for horses years before, and he led Pedro into one of them.

"Too bad there isn't any hay for him to sleep on," he said. "I'll get some tomorrow if I have to cut it myself. Let's go to the house and get a pail of water for him."

He opened the back door, which wasn't even locked, and the children followed him into the kitchen. When he had lighted an oil lamp he scanned the shelves of Mrs. Moody's pantry. "Ah, here are some Quaker Oats," he said with satisfaction. "They'll be awfully stale, but Pedro won't mind."

"He loves them," Kevin assured him.

Lucille gazed eagerly around the room, hardly noticing what the others said or did. She couldn't believe she was really inside the mysterious Moody house. The kitchen was low-ceilinged and small, with windows that looked up toward the street on one side and off over the marsh on the other. There was a cushioned rocking chair near the back windows. Mrs. Moody must have sat there to read and to look out on the marsh and the sea.

"There's a great stock of canned goods here," Mr. Lindsay observed. "I could live on it all winter if I could be satisfied with tuna fish and spaghetti and soup."

"Mrs. Moody was a hermit," Kevin said. "She never went shopping, or anything. They delivered her grocery orders from Phil's Market. I guess she kept lots of stuff on hand in case of bad weather when the grocery boy couldn't come."

"Her lawyer told me how solitary she was," Mr. Lindsay agreed. "I wonder why? Whatever happened to make her want to stay by herself all the time?"

The children shook their heads. "Nobody seems to know," Lucille said.

"She was a *real* hermit," Brent declared.

Mr. Lindsay laughed. His laugh, like his voice, was much louder and heartier than anyone expected from such a small man.

"If she had been a real hermit I don't believe she'd have got married," he said.

He stopped, suddenly, and picked up something from the floor near the kitchen table. He handed it to Lucille. "I guess this must be yours."

Lucille stared. It was a blue linen handkerchief. As she turned it in her hand she saw that there was a darker blue flower embroidered on one corner of it. It certainly didn't belong to *her*. But she knew she had seen one just like it somewhere. Oh, yes — it was Miss Rand who had one. The owner of The Blue Goose always kept a blue handkerchief like this sticking out of the pocket of her white uniform.

So it *had* been Miss Rand whom she had seen stealing up the lane a few minutes ago! She must have found the door unlocked and walked right into the kitchen. How had she dared? Had she known, before she came, that Mr. Lindsay was out?

"Do you know Miss Rand, the lady who owns The Blue Goose?" she asked curiously.

Mr. Lindsay shook his head. "I met her this noon, when I stopped there for lunch. But I didn't find her very friendly. She must be one of the many local people who don't think I have a right to the island."

Kevin and Brent opened the door and they all followed Mr. Lindsay back to the barn. A few minutes later they said good-bye to him and to Pedro and hurried up the lane.

"It's too bad people don't want Mr. Lindsay to stay here," Lucille said with a sigh. "Even Miss Rand thinks Clyde Moody should have the island." She told the boys about the blue handkerchief. "Miss Rand must have had a reason for sneaking into the house. Maybe she was hunting for something, the same as Clyde was when he was up in the barn. I wonder what it can be?"

"You should have told Mr. Lindsay it was her handkerchief," Brent said reprovingly. "If people are snooping around the place, he's got a right to know."

"The island is *his,* no matter what Clyde or Miss Rand or anyone else may say," Kevin insisted loyally.

"And it's Pedro's home, now," Lucille reminded them. "That's the important thing. We've got to help him keep it."

Friends—No Matter What

THURSDAY was a real Indian-summer day, so clear and mild it seemed a crime to have to stay in school. When the children got home that afternoon Brent and Kevin decided to go to the vacant lot to play football.

"We can't go to the island *every* day," Brent said.

Kevin noticed the disappointment in Lucille's gray-blue eyes and added, "Pedro doesn't need us now, and Mr. Lindsay may be busy."

They hurried away and left Lucille to eat her peanut-butter sandwich in a gloomy silence.

Her mother glanced out the kitchen window and said, "Pammy and Linda seem to be on their way to the library. Why don't you go with them? Haven't you some books you should return?"

Lucille shook her head, making believe her mouth was so full she couldn't talk. Mamma didn't know about the stupid Saturday Club and how stuck-up Pammy and Linda had been ever since they were invited to join it. It was a pity they were the only girls in Pinewood Acres who were her own age. Lucille had used to think they were dull, but it had certainly been better to have them for playmates than to have no one.

The new girl, Barbara Rosen, wasn't any help. She was too stiff and quiet. She didn't even *want* to make friends. Once when Lucille happened to sit beside her in the school bus, she had tried to get acquainted with her. She asked Barbara how she liked school and whether she had a bicycle. All the other girl answered was "Okay" and "Mm-hm." Then she turned her head and stared out the bus window as if she didn't want to talk. What could you do with a person like that?

"I'm going over to Salt Pond," Lucille told her mother, speaking brightly as if this were something she was really crazy about doing. "It's so warm I can take that old boat out and row around. I haven't done that since summer."

Salt Pond was a wide, shallow body of water on the inner marsh — the part that lay between the marsh road and the center of town. The pond wasn't deep enough to be dangerous and it was too boggy for swimming. Hardly anyone went there. To reach it Lucille had to walk to the far end of Pinewood Acres and down a dirt road. A footpath led to the pond.

By the time she reached the footpath she had begun to feel more cheerful. She loved to row and it would be fun to splash around in a boat again, with the warm sun shining on her head and shoulders. She heard the sound of a shotgun blast in the distance and was glad she didn't have to worry about that. Bird-hunting was forbidden on the inner marsh.

A few straggly bushes hid the pond from sight until Lucille came to the very end of the path and saw the water gleaming in the afternoon light. She stepped down to the shore and turned to look for the boat. At that moment she saw that someone had got there ahead of her.

"Oh — *drat!*" she muttered through clenched teeth, when she realized that the other person was Barbara Rosen. What was she doing here, anyway?

Barbara's back was turned and she didn't seem to be aware that Lucille had come. She had a handful of muddy pebbles which she was hurling, one at a time, into the pond. She threw fiercely, as if she were angry enough to want to hurt something. When her left hand was empty she rubbed it across her eyes, and sniffed.

Lucille was startled. Gee, Barbara was *crying!* What could have happened to make her feel so bad? She stepped backward toward the path, thinking she would slip away and leave the other girl alone. But Barbara whirled around at that instant and saw her.

Lucille couldn't help staring. Barbara's cheeks were streaked with dirt from the muddy stones she had been holding, and with tears. Her dark eyes were tearful, too, but they flashed angrily as she stared back at Lucille. "What are *you* doing here?" she demanded.

Lucille felt like apologizing even though she knew she had as much right to be there as Barbara had. "I — uh — walk over here — sometimes — to row on the pond," she explained, turning her eyes away from the other girl's face.

Barbara sniffed again. She pulled a handkerchief from her pocket and scrubbed at her wet cheeks with it. "I j-just get — lonesome," she muttered. "You and your Saturday Club are such snobs. Oh — I wish I hadn't ever come here to live!"

Lucille gazed at her in openmouthed astonishment. "I don't belong to that stupid club," she said.

"You don't?" It was Barbara's turn to stare. "Why, I thought you did. Why — you're smarter than most of the girls, and you're always in the plays and programs — I don't see why they wouldn't ask *you!*"

Her amazement at the idea soothed Lucille's hurt pride. Her admiring words helped, too.

"I don't know how they pick their members," she said, "and I don't care." She added, more honestly, "I mean, I'm *not going* to care. You were right — they *are* a bunch of snobs."

"I thought I was the only one they didn't ask," Barbara muttered. "But if they didn't ask you either — "

Lucille giggled. "If they didn't ask me they must be *really* dumb." Her gray-blue eyes sparkled and Barbara began to smile, too.

"I thought the only girls who weren't asked were the odd ones like Cindy Richter, who plays with the little second-grade kids, and Irma Jones who's such a spoiled brat," Barbara went on. She tossed her head. "I think it makes those girls feel important just to keep some of us out."

"Nuts to them," Lucille said airily. "Let's take the boat and row for awhile before the sun goes down and it gets too cold."

Barbara looked at the old boat pulled up among the reeds on the shore. It was muddy and it smelled of fish and bait and the salt flats.

"Is it — safe?" she asked doubtfully.

"Oh, sure. The pond's only about three feet deep.

And the boat's okay. I've rowed it lots of times."

Barbara didn't know how to row, but she took the oar Lucille handed her and climbed into the boat.

"You sit in the middle. I'll sit in back so I can steer. We have to paddle instead of rowing because there aren't any oarlocks," Lucille explained.

As she pushed the boat off and hopped in she thought to herself, "I wonder if Barbara and I can really be friends. Gee, I hope so. We wouldn't have to care about the old Saturday Club if we had each other to play with."

Barbara began to splash water all over the place, and the more she splashed, the more she laughed. "I've never done this before," she said. "It's lots more fun than riding in my uncle's motorboat, because there's something to do."

Lucille had plenty to do just to keep the boat from

going around in circles. But she enjoyed it, too. They were reaching the point where they paddled well together when a shout from the muddy bank startled them. Barbara dropped her oar and almost lost it.

"Hey, bring that boat ashore!"

Lucille exclaimed in a low voice, "It's George Turner. But this can't be *his* boat. His folks have a big one with a motor and everything."

George was dressed like a fisherman, wearing rough clothes and rubber boots that came up to his hips. He looked so scowling and unpleasant Lucille felt like rowing away from him, but she didn't dare. Unwillingly, she steered toward where he was standing.

"You're beginning to bug me," he told her angrily. "Hereafter, for Pete's sake, keep out of my hair!" He climbed into the boat, set some oarlocks in place, and began to row toward the creek that flowed out at the far end of the pond.

"It's getting late, anyway," Barbara said. "It was really time for us to go home."

"I still don't think the boat belongs to George." Lucille frowned. "I shouldn't have brought it back just because he told me to."

"I've seen him out fishing with that fellow whose family used to own Moody's Island," Barbara said. "Maybe he's going to meet him now. Maybe it's *his* boat."

Lucille's blue eyes grew thoughtful. "Clyde Moody? Hmm. Maybe it *is* his boat. He's no better than

George. I don't blame old Mrs. Moody for not leaving the island to him. I wouldn't have, either."

Barbara hesitated. "My father has heard a lot of talk about the man Mrs. Moody *did* leave the island to," she said. "His name is Lindsay. I guess he's no better than Clyde. He may even be worse. Some of Daddy's customers think he's a — " she lowered her voice to a whisper — "a spy."

Lucille knew that Barbara's father owned a clothing store on Main Street. He probably heard all the latest gossip there.

"Mr. Lindsay is no spy," she answered scornfully. She explained how she and the boys had met him and how he had saved Pedro. "We like him. He's a nice guy."

Barbara listened with a troubled face. "Even Mr. Estabrook thinks he must be a crook. He told Daddy he wrote to this Mr. Lindsay and offered to buy the island from him. He thought a stranger might have no use for the property. But Mr. Lindsay wouldn't sell. Mr. Estabrook thinks there must be some queer reason why he intends to keep it. Who would want to live in that run-down old place?"

"Mr. Estabrook shouldn't say he's a spy," Lucille declared. "I bet he was just mad because Mr. Lindsay wouldn't sell the island to him. He's used to running things his way around here."

"But that lonely island *would* be a good place for a spy to live," Barbara said. "He could have a radio and communicate with ships and submarines. My father says it really looks bad. How did a complete stranger ever get Mrs. Moody to leave her property to him in the first place? It seems as if there must be something wrong about him."

At first Lucille thought it was almost a joke. Mr. Lindsay — that funny, friendly little man — a spy! If someone couldn't find anyone more dangerous than he was to be a spy, she guessed nobody would need to worry.

But as she and Barbara walked along the road toward home in a companionable silence, she began to feel differently. She looked across the darkening marsh toward the sea. In the late light she could barely discern the outlines of Moody's Island. It was very lonely and secret. She admitted reluctantly to herself that if a spy *did* want to signal a ship by radio, or help a foreign agent steal ashore, that island would be a good place on which to do it.

She remembered Mr. Lindsay's sharp glance and cold voice when he spoke to Mr. Turner about Pedro. He had sounded dangerous *then.* Just because he was kind to animals wasn't enough to prove he was a really good person.

For a minute or two she felt cross with Barbara, as if the sudden uneasiness that had crept into her mind was her fault. She looked at the other girl's quiet, concerned face and changed her mind again. She liked her. They were going to be friends, *no matter what.*

Barbara said thoughtfully, "I wonder where George *was* going in that old boat? It's almost dark. I should think it was too late for him to go fishing."

Lucille was surprised that she hadn't thought of that herself. The creek into which he steered the boat ran under the marsh road bridge. From there it wound its way past Moody's Island. George could reach the island just about dark when Mr. Lindsay wouldn't see him. Was that what he — and maybe Clyde — were planning to do?

A Strange Request

THE WARM, GOLDEN WEATHER lasted all day Friday. Lucille took the bus to school so she could ride with Barbara. At recess time they walked around the playground arm in arm. They ignored the group of Saturday Club girls who were laughing and talking together about their plans for the following day.

"Marjorie's mother has invited them all to her house to lunch," Barbara said. "Then one of the other mothers is going to take them to Portland to a movie. They *do* have good times." Her voice sounded wistful.

Lucille sniffed and tossed her blond head. "Huh. They can't seem to do anything by themselves. All they do is get the different mothers to take them places. If I belonged to a club I'd want it to be one that did things *itself*."

"Like what?"

"Oh — bike rides and picnics and games. Stuff like that," Lucille replied.

Barbara sighed and looked over toward the group of club girls enviously, as if she thought they really had more fun. She didn't say anything. Her look and her silence nettled Lucille.

"Listen, I know something you and I could do tomorrow," she said. "We could ride over to Spruce Point and try to find the house where that famous artist used to live. You know — the one Miss Weeks is always talking about, in art class."

"Brooks Waldron," Barbara murmured thoughtfully.

"Yeah. Miss Weeks says we ought to be proud to live in the region he painted so many great pictures of. But I've never seen his studio nor more than a few of his pictures. Have you?"

"It would be a long ride. Spruce Point must be four miles or more from home."

"We could take our lunch and have a picnic over there, if the weather stays warm!" Lucille exclaimed. "Hey, that would be fun!"

"And I could take pictures of the house and the studio and everything." Barbara's voice began to sound excited, too. "I got a new camera for my birthday. Let's do it!"

They grew so much interested in the idea, they

didn't even notice that the Saturday Club girls had broken off their own chatter to look after them curiously.

Brent and Kevin were curious about the new friendship between the girls, too.

"I thought you said Barbara Rosen was snooty," Brent observed, when he and Kevin and Lucille were having their afternoon snack together at Kevin's house.

"Yeah, I thought you didn't like her," Kevin added.

"Well — now *you* know what thought did," Lucille said loftily. "Barbara is a very nice girl. I'd have invited her to go to the island with us this afternoon if she hadn't had her piano lesson."

There was no argument about going to see Pedro that day. None of them could wait any longer to see how he was getting on and to find out what Mr. Lindsay was doing.

They saw the donkey on the knoll behind the house when they were only halfway down the lane. As soon as he heard them coming he lifted his big gray head, twitched his ears, and began to hiccup. "Uh-*hee* uh-*hee* — "

The children dropped their bicycles on the lawn and ran toward the knoll as fast as they could go.

"Look at his feet!" Kevin cried. "They're normal. He can almost walk straight!"

Pedro did hobble on bent ankles as he came to meet them, but not nearly so badly as he had before. His hoofs had been trimmed down so that they looked like any donkey's hoofs.

"He isn't quite used to his nice new feet yet," Mr. Lindsay said, coming up the knoll after the children. "They're probably tender, after all the work Dr. Phillips did on them."

"He's free. You haven't got him tied to anything," Brent observed in surprise.

Lucille hugged the little burro joyfully. "Gee, Pedro, isn't it fun to wander around, and find grass and stuff to eat, and not be staked out in a muddy old cabbage patch?"

Mr. Lindsay rubbed the donkey's head. "He'll soon be trotting all over the place without a bit of trouble. Then you kids can ride him. There's even an old saddle in the barn you may be able to use. Come on, I'll show it to you."

He had cut the long grass around the house and strewed it on the floor of the stall to make Pedro more comfortable. Lucille noticed with approval the water dish and box of grain, too. There would be no need to worry about the little donkey anymore.

While the boys were examining the saddle, Mr. Lindsay said, "I do have a problem, though. I've got to go back to Lewiston for a few days to move my things out of my old apartment. I wondered if you children would take care of Pedro while I'm away?"

Kevin and Brent looked at each other gleefully.

"Gee, you bet!"

"Oh boy, we'll come every afternoon and feed him and let him out to get his exercise — "

"We'll be glad to," Lucille said, making sure the boys knew that *she* was included in the plan. "We'll keep an eye on the house, too." She remembered the blue handkerchief Miss Rand must have dropped on the kitchen floor and added, "You'll be sure to lock everything up, won't you?"

Mr. Lindsay's eyes twinkled as he glanced at Lucille's determined face. "I will. And I'll see that you get the key. Now let's go in the house and have a drink together. A house hasn't really been lived in, you know, until friends have been entertained there."

He led them through the kitchen to the front room with the bay window that gave the best view of Nine-Mile.

"This is going to be my studio," he explained. He had placed an oak dining table in front of the bay window. It held his typewriter and scattered papers already. "And see how I've cleaned off the bookshelves," he added proudly. "I'll be able to have all my books right at hand. This will be a great place to work. Pedro can look in the window and keep me company, if he wants to. I hope the ducks and herons and gulls will come close enough for me to watch them, too."

Kevin and Brent sat down on an old horsehair sofa and Lucille took the rocker near the hall door.

"I don't suppose any of you like Moxie, do you?"

Mr. Lindsay asked, as he started toward the kitchen.

"I do," Brent said quickly. "It's my favorite."

"Mine, too," Mr. Lindsay said with a grin.

He brought two Cokes and two Moxies on a tray, with paper napkins and glasses. "Because you're my first guests," he said. "It's a special occasion."

Lucille gazed around the room while the boys talked about Pedro and how they would ride him all over the island as soon as his feet were better. The furniture was old and shabby and the wallpaper was dark. She wondered if Mr. Lindsay would bring new furniture with him when he came back from Lewiston.

He laughed when she asked about it. "I haven't many possessions. Just clothes and books and my radio equipment. I can carry it all in my old car."

Lucille's gray-blue eyes darkened. She glanced at him questioningly. "Radio equipment?"

"I'm a ham operator. That means I can send and receive messages myself," he explained, "WAQ 54 — that's me. I'll be glad to be located on this island where I won't get much interference. I won't be bothering my neighbors' radio and TV reception, either. I have a friend on an island off Georgia that I talk to almost every day."

The boys were thrilled to hear about that. They begged to be shown how a ham operator worked so they could learn to send and receive messages. "It's something like a walkie-talkie, isn't it?" Kevin asked eagerly.

Lucille didn't pay any attention to the talk that followed. The two words — *radio equipment* — were enough to reawaken all the doubts she had felt when Barbara first told her story about Mr. Lindsay being a spy. Radio equipment would be the most important thing a man who was a spy would need.

She glanced with narrowed eyes at the table, placed so conveniently close to the window that looked across the marsh to the open sea. Mr. Lindsay might call it his studio, and spread his papers and books around. But wasn't it odd that a man whose main business was being a writer didn't even have a desk to bring to his new home? And didn't own any furniture except books and radio equipment that he could carry with him in his car?

She was so absorbed in these thoughts she didn't notice the sound of a car pulling up in the driveway. The loud knock on the back door startled them all. Mr. Lindsay hurried to the kitchen to answer it.

"I'm Sam Estabrook," a loud, familiar voice announced — much to the children's surprise. "And this is Clyde Moody, the last member of the family who used to own this island. I don't believe you two have met."

Mr. Lindsay said, "How do you do," in a guarded voice, and waited. The children waited, too, shrinking back into the part of the room that couldn't be seen from the kitchen doorway.

"Mind if we step in?" Mr. Estabrook asked in his

most jovial tone. "Clyde has a — uh — a favor he wants to ask of you."

"I'd like to look over the family papers and old pictures and things that my aunt must have left here in this house," Clyde muttered. "Those things can't be worth anything to you."

Mr. Estabrook added smoothly, "I thought you might be willing to bundle them up and let Clyde take them. After all, he's the only Moody still living. The only one who would value such personal family treasure. You understand, I'm sure."

"Well now, I'll tell you," Mr. Lindsay said slowly. "I'd want to look those things over myself before I parted with them. In her will the old lady left everything to me — lock, stock, and barrel. No mention was made of giving the family papers to her nephew. But I'm willing to hunt them up and go over them with Clyde, here, if he wants to come back in a week or two. That would give me time to see if there are any papers that I should keep — fire insurance policies, things like that, you know."

Lucille had to smile as she listened. Mr. Lindsay was smart, all right! He didn't let Sam Estabrook's smooth talk fool *him.*

Clyde spoke angrily to his companion.

"I *told* yuh," he snorted. "No use talking to a crook like *him* about anything — "

"Oh, come now," Mr. Estabrook interrupted hastily. "Getting angry isn't going to solve anything. I must say, Lindsay, I don't think you are being fair about this. It isn't easy for Clyde to come and ask a favor of you. You might at least go halfway and let him have the papers right now. He doesn't feel — uh — friendly enough to want to spend time looking over family souvenirs with you."

"I'll turn the stuff over to his aunt's lawyer, then," Mr. Lindsay suggested. "Clyde can go over the papers with him. I'll agree to that."

"Look, Lindsay — " Mr. Estabrook's voice began to sound angry — "you don't seem to realize what a rotten deal Clyde has had because of old Mrs. Moody's unreasonable decision to leave the family property to a stranger. You *were* a stranger, weren't you? You and Mrs. Moody never met?"

"We never met," Mr. Lindsay agreed.

"Well — there are plenty of people in this town who are wondering how you managed to get the property, I can tell you that. And Clyde *could* make serious trouble for you. If he went to court to contest the will it might cost you more than the place is worth to fight for it. You'd be smart to be a little more considerate when he asks you for a small favor."

"Aw, let's go, Sam," Clyde Moody growled. "I ain't gonna ask this guy for *nothin'*."

"Fred Waterman says the will is airtight and Clyde doesn't stand a chance of breaking it," Mr. Lindsay said to Mr. Estabrook. "And where would *he* get the money to fight a long court case? Am I to suppose that you would be backing him?"

After a moment of silence Sam Estabrook managed to laugh almost as heartily as ever. "We're getting way off the track," he said. "Clyde and I didn't mean to offend you, Lindsay. Since it's no use talking to you we'll run along. You'll hear from us later."

The kitchen door closed. Almost at once the lights of Sam Estabrook's car flashed through the bay window as he turned it around and headed up the lane. The front room seemed really dark when the lights disappeared. Mr. Lindsay lighted an oil lamp in the kitchen and called to the children to come out. "I don't believe those two men realized they had an unseen audience," he said with a chuckle.

"I'm glad you didn't give in to them," Brent told him. "I wouldn't trust either one as far as I could throw a piano."

"It seems mighty funny to me that Clyde would come here and ask for those papers," Mr. Lindsay said. "The house stood empty for six weeks after old Mrs. Moody died. He could have gotten in here then without much trouble. A simple skeleton key would have unlocked the back door. Don't tell me he wouldn't have walked in and taken the papers, if *he* was the one who wanted them."

"We heard him up in the barn one day," Kevin said. He told about the afternoon he and Lucille had explored the place. "At least, we thought it was Clyde. We weren't sure."

"So why should he come back *now* to ask for the family papers?" Behind his thick glasses Mr. Lindsay's eyes look puzzled.

"Maybe Mr. Estabrook wants something that Clyde didn't find," Lucille suggested.

Mr. Lindsay agreed that that was possible. "I hope nobody lets those two men know I'm going to be away," he added. "I wouldn't want Clyde to have another try at searching the house."

Lucille said suddenly, "We'd better go. It's almost dark outside."

The boys said they would be back tomorrow, but Lucille remembered that she was going to Spruce Point with Barbara. As they rode their bicycles up the lane she glanced back at the island and shivered. How would she and the boys dare to go there to care for Pedro when Mr. Lindsay was gone? She thought of the radio equipment he was going to bring back with him, and for a few uneasy moments she wished she had never come to Moody's Island at all.

On the Spruce Point Road

THERE WAS FROST in the air when Lucille set out for Barbara's house on Saturday forenoon. The two girls met halfway. Barbara flew along easily on a bicycle as new and colorful as Kevin's. As they turned onto the marsh road they saw the boys ahead of them on their way to Moody's Island.

"What are they going over there for?" Barbara asked when Brent and Kevin turned into the lane.

Lucille explained that they were going to take care of Pedro while Mr. Lindsay was away.

"The island looks like a good place for a murder," Barbara declared with a shiver. "I wouldn't want to live on it."

Lucille laughed. "Mr. Lindsay loves it." Her face grew sober as she realized suddenly how *much* he loved the island. It made a perfect place for his writing and his radio hobby. Pedro loved it, too, and they both deserved to keep it. She was sure they did, no matter what anybody said.

Spruce Point was a narrow ridge of land that reached across the marsh to the sea. It was covered with scrub oaks and spruce trees. A road ran along the middle of it out to a rocky headland. When the girls reached it their bikes began to rattle over frozen humps and bumps of earth.

"I'd forgotten there was construction on this road," Lucille said. "We'll have to go slowly here."

Work seemed to have stopped for the weekend. The big trucks and bulldozers were standing idle in a clearing in the trees. A little farther on, Barbara noticed three gulls, snowy white against the black roof of a tar-papered shack.

"I'm going to take a picture of them," she said, hopping off her bicycle.

Lucille clutched her arm. "Don't," she whispered sharply. She pointed to a mailbox beside the road with the name *Moody* printed on it in big letters. "This must be where Clyde lives. We can't stop here."

Barbara already had her camera set, so she snapped the picture anyway. Then she hopped back onto her bike and she and Lucille rode on with an extra burst of speed.

It was noon when they reached the village of Spruce Point. Smoke curled from the chimneys of the

fishermen's houses on the harbor side of the point, but the big cottages on the high ground were all closed. The road was so steep the girls had to get off and push their bicycles up to the top.

"What a view!" Barbara exclaimed. "No wonder Brooks Waldron had his studio here."

"We'd better find somebody who can tell us where his house is," Lucille suggested.

"Oh, let's find it ourselves! It would be more adventurous. You know what you said about the Saturday Club girls always letting other people do everything for them," Barbara reminded her.

Fir woods covered most of the headland. From the parking outlook where she was standing, Lucille could see the roof and upper story of a gray-shingled house that was taller than the trees around it and faced straight out to sea. "I bet that's the place," she said.

"Let's leave our bikes and walk up to it," Barbara suggested.

"Well, okay, only I'm going to take my lunch with me," Lucille said. "I'm starved. If that *is* Brooks Waldron's house, I'm going to eat right on the front steps. I guess that would be something to tell my grandchildren about!"

Barbara laughed. "I hope nobody's there. Brooks Waldron is dead, of course, but some of his family might still be around."

"Or his ghost," Lucille said with a giggle.

It was shadowed and still on the lane that led up to

the house. The girls were breathless from the climb when they finally arrived in front of it.

Barbara pointed to a bronze plaque under a front window:

The world-famous marine artist, Brooks Waldron, lived in this house from 1925 until his death in 1947. Many of his greatest paintings were of scenes in and around Spruce Point.

"We found it — all by our little selves!" she crowed.

They settled themselves on the sunny front steps to eat. Lucille had put up her own lunch, so there were no special surprises in hers. But Barbara's mother and her Aunt Sara had given her so many kinds of cookies and sandwiches she kept passing things to Lucille. She took a picture of her on the steps, too, with the lunch bags and Thermos bottles and sweaters spread out around her.

"I'd better not show it to Miss Weeks," she said with a grin. "She'd think we didn't show the proper respect for her favorite artist, eating lunch on his doorstep."

When they were done they left their things there and picked their way down to the shore. It was exciting to climb over the cliffs and the enormous rocks. Lucille gazed out to sea and said, "It looks like the paintings in Miss Rand's coffee shop."

While Barbara took more pictures, Lucille looked for smooth stones to add to her collection. Barbara found two unusual ones for her, but Lucille shook her head.

"I only collect feeling stones," she said. "They have

to be as smooth as satin — something like a horse chestnut when you first take it out of its shell. You can carry one in your pocket and rub your fingers over it. It helps when you feel nervous or just want to think."

Barbara laughed. "I never heard of feeling stones. It sounds kind of — queer."

"My father says the Chinese people have used them for hundreds of years, only they call them meditation stones. Here, try it." She handed Barbara a smooth black one hardly larger than a pebble.

"Hmm — it *is* smooth. It feels nice to run my fingers over it," Barbara agreed.

The afternoon was growing late when the girls climbed back up the hill. As they emerged from the woods they were startled to see a woman sitting on the steps where they had left their things. Their first thought was that one of the Waldron family must have returned. Would she be angry with them for trespassing? Lucille took a second look and exclaimed in relief, "Oh, it's only Miss Rand!"

Miss Rand smiled. "I was wondering who had the nerve to picnic right on Brooks Waldron's doorstep. I saw you two girls down on the rocks but I didn't recognize you."

Lucille explained about their art teacher who admired Brooks Waldron so much. "So we thought we'd find his house and take pictures of it," she said.

Miss Rand nodded approvingly. "I'm glad you have a teacher who appreciates him. I've always loved his paintings, myself. I have several of them in my shop. Haven't you noticed?"

"I noticed there were pictures of the ocean and fishermen and stuff, but I didn't know who painted them," Lucille replied.

"They are only reproductions, of course, not the original paintings," Miss Rand admitted with a sigh. She explained that she often drove over to Spruce Point, just to look off at the ocean and try to see it as the artist must have seen it. "It rests me," she said.

She walked with them to the parking outlook where they had left their bikes. The girls were so weary they almost wished they could ride back in her car.

Lucille sighed when she saw it disappear around a curve at the bottom of the hill. "I'm afraid it will be dark before we get home."

"What do we care? We've had heaps of fun," Barbara said with satisfaction.

They rode fast on the first part of the way, but when they reached the stretch of new road with its humps and bumps, they had to slow down to a crawl. The sun slid behind a cloud bank and the wooded road began to grow dark. The girls stopped chattering and tried to hurry in spite of the roughness of the way.

As they approached the clearing where the big trucks and bulldozers were parked, two men suddenly stepped into the road not far ahead of them. They didn't notice the girls in the tree-shadowed curve. They were carrying a heavy package between them

and they walked with bent heads, intent on their work.

"It's George Turner again," Lucille whispered. "And Clyde Moody."

She and Barbara drew their bicycles as far off the road as they could and waited. George and Clyde walked to the edge of the road and started to climb down the bank to the marsh.

"Watch it!" George exclaimed. "Don't stumble, whatever you do."

A moment later the girls heard the creaking of oars in oarlocks and Lucille whispered, "They've got a boat, thank goodness. We won't have to worry about their seeing us on the road."

They hopped back onto their bicycles and raced over the bumps, not caring *how* much they were shaken up.

"What could they have been carrying?" Barbara

asked, when they reached the familiar marsh road and could see the boat far out on the creek.

Lucille shrugged. "Probably beer or whiskey or whatever it is they drink. They wouldn't be so careful of anything else."

"That isn't the same boat George took away from us at the pond," Barbara pointed out. "It's blue, isn't it?"

They turned for another look, but it was so far away they couldn't be sure what color it was, in the dim light.

Lucille frowned. It didn't make sense for those two to carry stuff from Clyde's shack to George Turner's house in a boat. They could have used the farm truck or Clyde's old car for that.

She began to consider the events of the afternoon. Miss Rand had been at Spruce Point and had driven back over the road just before George and Clyde appeared with their bundle. The rowboat they were using might be blue — like the shutters on The Blue Goose. Could it be Miss Rand's boat? Was she mixed up with Clyde and George in whatever they were doing?

"We'd better hurry," Barbara murmured. "My folks will be worried if I don't get home soon."

As they flew past Moody's Island they saw the lamplight shining warmly from the kitchen windows. Lucille thought of Mr. Lindsay bustling around getting supper, and of Pedro, safe and happy in his stall in the barn. Neither of them had any idea that George and Clyde were out on the marsh, not far from their island.

"Who is there to help them keep their new home," she asked herself, "except Barbara, and the boys, and me?"

The Lost Ring

BRENT was talking loudly when Lucille came down to breakfast on Sunday morning.

"At the movies last night all the kids were saying that Mr. Lindsay is a spy," he sputtered. "They say that's why he wants to live on a lonely island. Gee, Dad, anybody who ever met Mr. Lindsay would know that wasn't true. He's an awful nice guy."

"Nice guys have turned out to be spies before this," Daddy answered, half-jokingly, "but I don't believe your Mr. Lindsay is one. People talk about him because they don't like the fact that Mrs. Moody left the island to him for no reason at all. They think he must have tricked her into doing it. Even though they don't respect Clyde Moody very much, they think the island should have gone to him. That's why they all make all this talk about Mr. Lindsay."

"It's no reason to call him a spy," Brent declared hotly.

"No. But that's an easy way to discredit a person these days. That's why people do it."

"Barbara heard that story, too," Lucille told them. "Her father has heard it so often he thinks there must be something to it. You know, people always say 'Where there's smoke, there's fire.' But I don't believe it."

"It's a good thing Mr. Lindsay doesn't know what they're saying," Brent went on. "He thinks this is a wonderful town. That's why he's in such a hurry to move out of his city apartment and bring his things back here. He's leaving this afternoon. Kevin and I are going over to say good-bye and play with Pedro for a while."

"Barbara and I are going, too," Lucille said quickly.

She washed the breakfast dishes while Mamma was getting Debbie ready for Sunday School. As she swished the cups and saucers through the water she gazed out the window and thought about Mr. Lindsay. He was a nice, kindhearted man, and she wasn't going to believe anything bad about him unless she absolutely had to.

The Indian-summer weather had slipped away and the afternoon was gray and cold. As they started off on their bicycles, Kevin turned his round, cheerful face to look up at the clouds. "We'll be lucky if it doesn't rain."

"I had to wear my raincoat, you might know," Barbara said. "My aunt wouldn't let me go without it."

The boys were in a hurry. They were afraid Mr. Lindsay would leave for Lewiston early, to get ahead of the rain. Barbara had no trouble keeping up with them, but Lucille, as usual, had to pump until she was out of breath.

They were surprised to see Mr. Lindsay's old car parked outside The Blue Goose. He must be having dinner there.

"I think we should go in," Kevin said, after a moment's hesitation. "He's probably going right on to Lewiston from here."

They found their small, bespectacled friend perched on a stool at the counter, chatting amiably with Miss Rand. He was delighted to see them. Lucille introduced Barbara to him.

"Makes me feel good to know I already have a group of friends to see me off," he said.

Miss Rand smiled. "I hope you include me in that." Turning to the children she added, "Sit down and have a hot drink with us just to wish Mr. Lindsay a good trip."

She set out cups of hot chocolate for the children and even poured some coffee for herself.

Mr. Lindsay lifted his cup. "Happy landings to you, too, Miss Rand," he said gallantly.

Lucille gulped and coughed at that. The picture of solid, steady Miss Rand making a happy landing, like a bird alighting on the marsh, made her want to giggle. Miss Rand and Mr. Lindsay, together, were certainly an odd pair.

"I left Pedro out on the knoll," Mr. Lindsay told the children. "I hated to shut him in so early. Will you put him into his stall before you leave?" He explained to Miss Rand that they would be looking after the donkey while he was gone.

"I'd be glad to keep an eye on things, too," she said. "You — uh — you might want to leave your house key with me."

"Well, thank you very much, but the children will need the key. They'll have to get water and food for Pedro, you see."

Lucille had been surprised at the friendliness Miss Rand was showing. Only a few days ago, when he ate lunch here, Mr. Lindsay had thought she didn't seem to like him. Could Miss Rand have taken this new attitude just because she planned to ask for his key?

Her uneasy feeling about the coffee shop owner lingered in her mind after Mr. Lindsay departed and she and Barbara and the boys were riding down the lane. She remembered the day when they first led Pedro to the island. She had seen Miss Rand, that day, sneaking up the lane and scurrying out of sight. It was *her* blue handkerchief Mr. Lindsay found on his kitchen floor, afterward. And she had been on the Spruce

Point Road yesterday, just before Clyde and George stepped out of the woods with their bundle. The blue boat they were using might even have been hers.

Lucille shook her head in bewilderment. There were just too many things about Miss Rand that she couldn't explain.

"I feel sorry for Mr. Lindsay," Barbara said when they were almost to the island. "He likes this place so much, and he *is* nice."

"Why should you be sorry for him?" Brent demanded.

She hesitated. "Well, my father hears all the gossip at his store, you know. He says people are sure Clyde Moody will get this island, in the end. Mr. Lindsay won't be able to keep it."

"But the lawyer told him the will was perfectly clear. The place does belong to him," Brent protested.

"The will may be all right," Barbara said slowly. "It isn't that. Clyde has a new story now. He says the island didn't belong to Mrs. Moody in the first place, so she couldn't leave it to Arnold Lindsay or anyone."

The other three children stared at her.

"Didn't belong to Mrs. Moody?" Kevin asked incredulously.

She shook her head. "Clyde says his uncle was never married to her. John Moody went away on a trip and brought this woman back with him, years ago. Everyone thought she was his wife, but Clyde says she was just a hired housekeeper for his uncle. He says there is no record, anywhere, that proves they were married. The island belonged to John Moody and now it belongs to Clyde because he's the only member of the family left."

"Mrs. Moody *wasn't* Mrs. Moody?" Lucille faltered.

Barbara shook her head again, unhappily. "Not if Clyde's story is true. He's telling everyone, now, that he would have claimed the property right after his uncle died, only he didn't like to kick the old lady out of the only home she ever had."

"Well, that's a crazy story," Brent declared indignantly, "and I don't believe a word of it. I bet Sam Estabrook thought it up. He's the one who's dying to get the island. Remember how he tried to persuade Mr. Lindsay to give all of the old lady's papers to Clyde? I bet he was afraid there might be a marriage certificate, or some other papers that would prove she was married to John Moody, still kicking around the house."

Kevin agreed with that. "It makes sense. Clyde would never have thought up such a clever way to claim the island, by himself. I bet that's what he was hunting for the day Lucille and I heard him up in the barn loft. Sam must have told him to look for the marriage license and destroy it."

"Well, they couldn't have found it!" Lucille exclaimed. "If they had they wouldn't have come and asked Mr. Lindsay for the family papers."

They heard a loud "Hee-*Haw!*" from Pedro at that moment. He came trotting down toward the lane to greet them. He walked easily, hardly bending his ankles at all.

"We'll soon be able to ride him," Kevin said.

Brent scowled. "Yeah — if Mr. Lindsay gets to stay here."

Barbara's news made them heavyhearted. They sat on the front steps for a while, thinking things over. They were so quiet that Pedro finally gave up hope of being petted and wandered back to the knoll.

As Lucille gazed over the marsh she suddenly remembered the blue boat Clyde and George Turner had used last night. She told the boys what she and Barbara had seen. "The boat was blue like the shutters on the coffee shop," she said. "Does Miss Rand have one like that?"

The boys didn't know.

"I don't see why everybody wants to help Clyde get this island," Brent muttered, "the Turners and Mr. Estabrook, and maybe Miss Rand. Even the people who gossip about Mr. Lindsay being a spy are helping Clyde, in a way."

"I wish *we* could help Mr. Lindsay," Kevin sighed.

After another brief silence Lucille asked, "Who has the key to the house?"

Kevin pulled it out of his pocket. "I have. Why?"

"We could look around in there," she answered thoughtfully. "If Mrs. Moody *was* Mrs. Moody the marriage certificate must be somewhere. Clyde may come back while Mr. Lindsay's gone. He may find it himself, if we don't beat him to it."

Barbara's face looked worried as she considered the idea, and Kevin's blue eyes widened in alarm. It was Brent who jumped up from the steps and said, "Let's try, anyway. Mr. Lindsay wouldn't mind if we searched his house. He knows we are on his side in this trouble."

They went around to the back door, opened it, and slipped into the kitchen. It was so quiet there that the ticking of the mantel clock sounded like a beating drum.

Brent led the way to the tiny front hall. "Let's see what's upstairs, first. We can search this floor anytime, but the bedrooms — well, I'd sort of hate to be caught up there."

There were only two rooms upstairs. Mr. Lindsay had been using one, and the other seemed to be a storeroom.

"We'll take his room," Lucille said. "You boys can search the closed-up one."

She and Barbara stepped nervously inside. Barbara tiptoed to the old-fashioned chest of drawers and pulled it open. Lucille looked into the closet where some of Mrs. Moody's dresses and skirts still hung. It made her feel sad to rummage among them and to examine the shelves where some of her shoes and other belongings were neatly stored away.

They spent a long time going over shelves and drawers and looking into a few cartons on the closet floor. They even turned the mattress on the bed, and then had to pull the sheets and blankets back and make it up again.

"Nothing," Barbara said gloomily. "Just — nothing."

The boys hadn't had any better luck in the musty storeroom. "The trunks are full of clothes, and there are stacks of magazines and old books. But there aren't any papers, not even a letter, anywhere," Kevin said in a discouraged tone of voice.

They trooped downstairs. The boys opened a door that led to the dark cellar.

"Hand me Mr. Lindsay's flashlight from the sink shelf," Brent said to Barbara.

"You aren't going down *there!*"

"We've got to," Kevin told her. He and Brent descended the shaky stairs, while the girls peered nervously after them. They were only gone about two minutes.

"There isn't anything in the cellar," Brent said, closing the door behind him and returning the flashlight to its place. "Just a dirt floor and a couple of bins where people used to store apples and vegetables, I guess. I don't believe Mrs. Moody ever used it."

Kevin sighed. "Everything is so clean and orderly in this house, it doesn't seem much like the house a real hermit would live in."

"I told you Mrs. Moody wasn't one," Lucille reminded him. "She was just an ordinary old lady who happened to like to live alone."

She and Barbara searched the kitchen while the boys went over the front room that Mr. Lindsay called his studio. They found dishes and towels and kettles — all the usual kitchen equipment — and hardly anything else.

On a small shelf near the window where Mrs. Moody's rocking chair stood there were three or four books. Lucille looked them over carefully. The first two were cookbooks and the third was a sort of scrapbook full of newspaper clippings of poems and things. But the very last one she opened was a thick notebook in which the old lady seemed to have kept a record of the different birds and flowers she had seen on the marsh, and even of the weather. The notebook covered years of observation of the seasons and the living creatures around the island.

"Didn't she write anything about herself or her husband — I mean, Mr. Moody?" Barbara asked.

"Maybe I'd find something if I had time," Lucille said. She skimmed the handwritten pages while Barbara continued to search the kitchen. Once in a while she found mention of some personal experience, like ordering a new coat or starting a flower garden.

Suddenly a note dated almost three years before caught her eye.

"Lost my wedding ring today while cleaning the

kitchen," it read. "Hunted everywhere, but couldn't find it."

In the pages that followed the old lady wrote of having looked again and again for the ring but she never mentioned that she had found it.

Lucille called Barbara and the boys and read the account of the lost ring to them. "Wouldn't her wedding ring be proof that she and Mr. Moody were married?" she asked.

The boys didn't think so, but Barbara said thoughtfully, "Sometimes people have their initials and the date of their marriage engraved on the inside of their wedding rings. If Mrs. Moody's had that, it ought to prove something."

"She lost it while she was cleaning the kitchen," Lucille murmured, gazing around the fast-darkening little room. "Gee, if we took rags and brooms and cleaned it ourselves — if we looked in every crack and every corner — "

"We might find it!" Barbara exclaimed.

Kevin shook his head. "I'm afraid it's too late. The old lady did her best and *she* couldn't find it."

"It must be here somewhere, though," Brent said, "unless she lost it down the sink drain or somewhere like that."

Lucille swung her hair back from her dusty face and declared firmly, "We'll come back after school tomorrow and go over this kitchen with a fine-tooth comb!"

They hurried to carry water and oats to Pedro's stall and to shut him in safely. Then they started home. Though it was dark and cold and they hadn't found anything worth finding, they felt a new hopefulness. The lost wedding ring *might* turn up. They didn't need to give up until they had really tried to find it.

Where There's Smoke

MONDAY was a dismal, lowering day. The clouds grew darker every hour and the wind grew colder. A storm seemed to be blowing up. It was no kind of weather for bicycle-riding over the lonely marsh, but the children were determined to go to the island before the rain began. The boys had to feed Pedro, anyway, and Lucille was allowed to go with them. Barbara was the one who almost had to stay home.

"I had to *cry,*" she said unhappily when she came flying into the Pierces' yard on her bike. "My folks always give in if I cry. But they are sure I'll get pneumonia and they'll worry all the while I'm gone. It takes the fun out of things."

The wind was so cold the children were chilled to the bone in spite of their fast pedaling along the road. They would have liked to stop at The Blue Goose to warm their hands and feet, but they couldn't take the time. They were afraid the rain would start before they had a chance to search for the lost wedding ring.

The boys carried oats and water to Pedro first of all, and let him out to roam the yard while they were in the house.

"We've got to go over every inch of this kitchen just as if we were cleaning it," Lucille said, as soon as they opened the door. "That's what Mrs. Moody was doing when she lost her ring. I've brought some old rags we can use."

She set the boys to work wiping the woodwork around the windows and doors. "Look in every crack where the ring could possibly have fallen," she said. "And when you get done you can start dusting the furniture — even the stove."

She and Barbara went into the pantry and began removing dishes from the shelves. They looked into each cup, bowl, pitcher, and teapot, and felt along the edges and into the corners of the shelves. The pantry was so cold they were glad to work hard and fast. They had to stamp their feet and stretch up and down on their tiptoes every few minutes to keep them from freezing.

"I think there's some kind of a conspiracy going on around here to get this house and island away from Mr. Lindsay," Lucille declared, as she knelt to pull pots and pans off of a low shelf. "Even respectable people like Sam Estabrook and Miss Rand seem to be mixed up in it."

"George Turner's in the conspiracy, too," Brent called from the kitchen. "He's hanging around with Clyde all the time. You never know what a couple of tough guys like them may do next. They sure would like to get Mr. Lindsay out of here."

"That gossip about his being a spy is the worst thing," Kevin said angrily. "If Mr. Lindsay hears that he may not even want to stay in this town."

"I sure hope he doesn't tell anyone else that he's a ham radio operator — at least, not until this trouble blows over," Brent added. "His radio equipment would really make people think he was a spy."

He and Kevin fell to work on the old black stove. It had many dark openings to be examined. The girls continued the long task of dusting every dish and package and kettle in the pantry. For a while they worked in silence with only the roar of the wind around the corners of the house and the clatter of stove lids in the kitchen to break it.

All at once Lucille became aware of a cheerful snapping sound coming from the other room. She stepped to the doorway and felt a slight, comforting warmth.

"You've got a fire!" she exclaimed.

Her brother nodded. "Darned right we have. We don't need to freeze, do we? Mr. Lindsay wouldn't mind if we lighted a fire, as long as we're careful."

"But Miss Rand or somebody on the marsh road may see the smoke! What will we say if she comes down here to find out about it?"

Brent peered from the window. "The sky is so dark the smoke will hardly show. Miss Rand will be busy getting supper for her customers. She'll never notice. And other people don't know Mr. Lindsay is gone. They'll think it's *his* fire."

The girls stood beside the stove for a minute to warm their hands. The water in the teakettle began to hum and hiss, and Barbara suggested daringly, "Why don't we make some cocoa? There's plenty of stuff on the pantry shelves. Mr. Lindsay wouldn't care. We could tell him about it when we see him."

The work became a party after that. While Barbara made the cocoa, Lucille toasted two big doughnuts which she found in the bread box. "They'd be too stale for Mr. Lindsay to eat by the time he got back," she said, as she cut them in halves and put them on a plate.

They pulled chairs close to the stove and sat with their feet pressed against the warm black metal.

"Where in heck can that wedding ring be?" Kevin asked with a frown.

Barbara sighed. "Maybe it got loosened on Mrs. Moody's finger while she had her hands in water. It could have slipped off into her scrubbing pail and she could have thrown it out on the ground or down the sink when she dumped the water out."

The others admitted gloomily that that could have happened. But there was always a chance that it hadn't. The ring might be pushed into some crevice almost under their very noses.

While they sipped their cocoa they peered into the dark corners of the room. Shadows were deepening so it would hardly be any use to continue the search. The mantel clock suddenly struck four loud, fast notes and the sound made them all jump.

A different sound followed close on the echo of the clock's striking. It was a hollow *whoo-ooo-oooo* that came from somewhere outside — a windy kind of sound, yet the children knew, without a moment's questioning, that it wasn't the wind. It seemed more like the cry of a screech owl in one of the tall trees.

"The Moody noises!" Brent cried.

"We might have known we'd hear them," Lucille added in a whisper, "with a storm about to begin."

Brent set his cup down on the end of the stove with a clatter. He grabbed Kevin by the shoulder. "Come on! Let's go see if we can find out where they're coming from!"

Before the girls had time to realize they would be left alone, he and Kevin disappeared through the back door.

Barbara and Lucille gulped the rest of their cocoa and carried the cups and saucers to the sink. They rinsed them and put them away. Then they returned to the stove, hovering over it as if they thought its warmth could stop their nervous shivering. The wailing *whoo-ooo-oo* that kept rising and falling in the dusk outside the house made them cold with fright. They heard Pedro *uh-hee*-ing loudly near the door. Evidently the noises were making him nervous, too.

"It's too dark to stay another minute," Barbara whispered finally. "Let's put things back on the pantry shelves and get out of here."

Without even trying to remember where the different dishes were supposed to go, the girls began piling them on the shelves. A stack of glass sauce dishes almost slipped from Barbara's stiff fingers, but she managed to catch them.

When they finished, Lucille went to look at the stove to make sure the fire was out. She glanced at the books on the kitchen shelf and hurriedly snatched Mrs. Moody's diary from among them. "I'm going to take it home and see if I can find any more clues," she whispered.

Breathlessly she and Barbara opened the back door and stole outside. They both let out startled shrieks as Pedro brayed loudly almost into their ears. He had been waiting for them right at the door.

Lucille put her arm around his neck and led him toward the barn. She and Barbara hated to go into the dark building, but they had to act calm so the little animal wouldn't be frightened.

"You'll be safe and warm here, Pedro," Lucille assured him in a firm voice. "Don't worry about the queer noises. You'll have to get used to them if you're going to live on Moody's Island."

Then the girls hurried back outdoors. They gazed around the yard, but the boys were nowhere in sight. With each loud, long-drawn-out *who-ooo* that rose in the air they felt more and more like grabbing their bicycles and fleeing from the island without waiting for anyone.

Lucille swallowed hard and managed to give a quavering shout. "Brent! Kevin! Where are you?"

There was no answer — nothing but the swoop of the wind and the hollow sound of the Moody noises.

The girls linked arms and shouted together. After a moment Barbara exclaimed thankfully, "Oh — there they come!"

The boys appeared at the corner of the barn. They didn't answer the girls' shouts, and they approached so slowly it seemed as if they didn't want to meet them. Their faces looked disturbed.

"Did you find out what makes the noises?" Lucille asked.

Brent shook his head. Kevin fumbled in his pocket for the key and went over to lock the door.

"We put Pedro in his stall," Barbara said.

Lucille continued to stare at the boys. "What's the *matter* with you?" she demanded at last. "You both look terrible."

"We went all over the island looking for the place

the noises come from," Kevin told them. "We went up on the knoll, and down to that old boat house by the landing — "

"And in the carriage shed behind the barn," Brent interrupted. "We found something there, all right."

"*What?*" the girls demanded, staring.

"We were looking in the old wagons. We thought there might be a piece of pipe or something the wind was blowing into — "

"And we found a box full of sticks of dynamite!" Brent muttered. "It was in one of the wagons. Mr. Lindsay's name and address were printed on it, too."

"Why should he need a box of dynamite?" Kevin asked unhappily. "What's he going to do with it?"

The feeling of friendship and trust that the children had felt for Mr. Lindsay began to ebb and fade as slowly and reluctantly as the afternoon light was ebbing from the marsh that surrounded them.

"Dynamite — and radio equipment — " Barbara murmured. "Gee, it seems as if people must have been right about him. He must be a spy — or something."

"I guess they knew more about him than we did. Probably there *was* something crooked in the way he got this island from poor Mrs. Moody. 'Where there's smoke, there's fire,' " Lucille quoted dolefully.

They heard a pleading *Uh-hee* from the barn, and the expressions on their faces grew even more unhappy. Pedro was there, settled in his quiet, lonely stall. And that box of dynamite was in the carriage shed only a few feet away from him. It might have been better for him if he had been left in the Turner's cabbage field.

They picked up their bicycles without another word and started slowly up the lane to the road.

Danger—Keep Out!

THE WEIRD WHOOO-OOO-ING of the Moody noises followed the children as they rode slowly up the lane. Even when they were halfway home they could hear the ghostly sound in the distance. It seemed to be following them, warning them to keep away from the island.

"We really shouldn't have hunted for that ring, or had a fire, or made cocoa," Lucille said to Barbara. "We shouldn't have got mixed up in Mr. Lindsay's business at all."

"We had to feed Pedro," Kevin reminded her. "And Mr. Lindsay gave us the key to his house."

"Maybe he wanted Miss Rand and other people to know we'd be over there a lot. He might have thought it would keep everyone else away," Brent suggested.

Barbara said in a small, scared voice, "What about the dynamite? We can't forget that. We've got to tell *someone* about it, haven't we?"

For a few moments nobody answered her question. They had all agreed to keep their knowledge of Mr. Lindsay's radio equipment a secret so people wouldn't be suspicious of him. But the dynamite was a different story. It was dangerous.

"Just the same," Kevin said stubbornly, "I hate to tell. Mr. Lindsay may have some perfectly good use for that stuff. I think we should wait until he comes back before we say anything to anyone."

"It's only fair to give him a chance to explain," Brent agreed.

"But the dynamite might explode," Lucille protested.

Brent scoffed at that. "Sticks of dynamite don't explode by themselves. You have to use caps and a fuse to set them off."

Kevin added, "We didn't run away from the carriage shed because we were afraid of an explosion. We just felt bad to think Mr. Lindsay must be doing something wrong — must be a spy, the way people said he was."

When the children separated, near their homes, they agreed to keep silent for two or three days. Surely it could wait that long.

The storm that had been threatening all afternoon began in earnest that night. The heavy wind and rain beat down so hard the marsh grass was flattened by morning and the creeks were swollen with dark, rushing water. It continued to rain all day Tuesday, too. The children didn't even try to go to the island to feed Pedro. He would have to get along with what food and water he had left.

Lucille curled up on her bed Tuesday evening, and opened the worn old notebook that was Mrs. Moody's diary. The rainy, gloomy night seemed a good time to read it.

"I don't know why I should bother, though," she said to herself. "If Mr. Lindsay is really a crook or a spy I don't want to help him keep the island. If he is, it doesn't matter whether we find the lost wedding ring or not."

The crowded handwriting was hard to read. Almost all the pages were filled with descriptions of the marsh birds and flowers. Mrs. Moody seemed to have spent most of her time watching them. She would write two or three pages telling about a goose whose wing had been injured in a storm, and how she fed it until it was well and able to fly away. The diary was full of things like that.

Lucille read until she was sleepy, without finding any mention of old John Moody, or of Mr. Lindsay, or anything that would help to explain the curious events that had been happening ever since Mrs. Moody's death.

She laid the diary down with a sigh. It began to seem as if nobody would ever know the real truth about the strange old lady, or her real reason for leaving the island to a man she had never met.

When Lucille and Barbara reached school on Wednesday morning and were hanging up their coats in the cloak room they couldn't help becoming aware of the giggling and whispering among the Saturday Club girls. They were excited about a birthday party they were going to that afternoon. It came to Lucille with a sudden shock that it was Pammy Clark's birthday they were talking about.

Lucille had been invited to Pammy's party every year since she had lived at Pinewood Acres. But this year it seemed that only the Saturday Club members were going. Lucille didn't really want to be at the party with them, but the feeling of being left out disturbed her just the same.

"Pammy wasn't much of a friend," she said scornfully to Barbara, as they walked into their classroom.

She found herself thinking about it many times during the day. Friends ought to be faithful and stick together even against a whole clubful of girls. She hoped she and Barbara would be like that. Brent and Kevin were real friends, even though they did squabble over little things now and then. Brent wouldn't have dreamed of joining a group that would leave Kevin out.

As she thought about other people who were loyal to each other, the image of Mr. Lindsay, with his bald head and spectacles, flashed into her mind. She saw him perched at the counter in The Blue Goose, beaming with pleasure as he spoke of having a group of good friends here already.

"We haven't been very loyal to *him,*" she thought uncomfortably.

Had they been wrong to let that hidden box of dynamite convince them he was doing something bad? There could be plenty of good uses for dynamite, couldn't there?

During the study hour, that afternoon, she went to the library shelf and looked up *dynamite* in the encyclopedia. She found a full-page illustration of its various uses: for boring tunnels, breaking log jams, building new roads, digging out boulders and tree stumps, and destroying old buildings.

She took the book back to her desk. Resting her round chin in her hands, her light hair falling around her face, she stared at the pictures thoughtfully. Mr. Lindsay couldn't want to bore a tunnel — not on that low, marshy island. He had no reason for digging out boulders or tree stumps. He wasn't going to build a road. And if he did want to get rid of one or two of the old buildings, he could tear them down easily enough. He wouldn't need dynamite to do it. No, she couldn't think of a single one of these regular uses of dynamite that would explain why he needed it.

As she continued to frown at the encyclopedia page, one picture caught her interest. It was of a road-building crew blasting a stone ledge out of the way. Some of the machines looked like those she and Barbara had seen on the Spruce Point Road.

A light seemed to flash on in her mind that very instant. George Turner and Clyde Moody had come out of the woods right near the clearing where those trucks and bulldozers had been parked. They were carrying something they had to be terribly careful about. She had taken it for granted that it was bottles of whiskey which they were afraid of breaking. But what if it had been sticks of dynamite, instead? They had taken it in the boat, just as it was getting dark. *They* could have hidden it in the carriage shed on Moody's Island!

For a minute she felt sure she had found the true explanation. She was so happy she felt like skipping as she returned the encyclopedia to the library shelf.

But a sober second thought made her spirits sink again. The men who were rebuilding the road certainly wouldn't leave a box of dynamite sticks lying around where George and Clyde could help themselves to it. Oh dear, maybe that nice, logical explanation wasn't right after all.

She decided not to say anything until she could talk to Barbara and the boys together. When she got off at her corner with Brent and Kevin she told Barbara to hurry back as fast as she could. "We're all going to the island to feed Pedro, you know."

It made her feel hungry herself, just to think of the little donkey's having gone without food for two days. She and Brent gobbled their drinks and cookies as fast as they could and hurried out to meet their friends.

Lucille told them her idea about the dynamite and where Clyde and George could have got it, as soon as they were all together on their way toward the island.

Kevin almost tipped his bicycle over in his excitement. "Hey, I bet that *is* where the dynamite came from! I bet Clyde and George *did* put it there!" He turned to Brent. "Remember last summer when our Scout Patrol took a hike to Scarborough? We went over a road that was under construction and we saw a wooden shack that had DANGER — HIGH EXPLOSIVES printed on it. Mr. Tobey said dynamite was kept in there."

"Yeah!" Brent got excited, too. "The work on the Spruce Point Road isn't finished yet. There may be a dynamite shack somewhere along it. Clyde would know. He lives over there."

"We ought to go and see," Kevin declared.

"But it's a long way to that new road," Barbara protested. "And what good would it do just to find the shack?"

"Why, heck, it's the only way we can be sure we're right. If we find a storage shed for dynamite near the place where you saw George and Clyde on Saturday, we'll know they must have been the ones who left the stuff in the carriage shed."

"And put Mr. Lindsay's name on the box," Brent added. "That was a dirty trick. I bet they were just hoping someone would find it and think he put it there."

"That was what *we* thought," Kevin said guiltily.

They had to ride faster than ever, because they had to get back to the island to feed Pedro and still get home before dark. The air was mild and calm, after the storm, but the flattened grass and the muddy, swollen creeks were discouraging to look at.

"Pedro will be starved to death," Lucille muttered. She thought of letting the boys ride ahead to look for the dynamite shack while she and Barbara went to the island and fed him. But when she saw Mr. Lindsay's house and the other buildings, rain-blackened and deserted, she felt scared. It would be safer for the four of them to stick together.

They pedaled the last mile in grim silence. Work on the new road had stopped during the long days of rain, so there were no workmen there. The children were thankful for that. They laid their bicycles down in the clearing where the bulldozers and trucks stood. Brent and Kevin ran around the machines and stopped at the edge of the woods.

"There it is!" Kevin shouted triumphantly.

They all stood silent for a moment, staring at the small shed hardly more than three feet square. Red-painted letters on the side of it read DANGER — KEEP OUT!

"There's a padlock on the door," Barbara faltered. "A big, heavy one."

"Clyde and George couldn't have opened that, could they?" Lucille asked.

The boys went up to the shack and examined the padlock.

"Look at the scratches in the wood all around it," Brent said. "Hey — I bet they pried it off and got the door open. Then they screwed it back in place again."

Kevin drew in his breath with a gulp. "That's it! Gee, Brent — what do we do now?"

Lucille looked from the boys' flushed faces to Barbara's pale one, and to the dark, dripping woods behind them. She began to shiver.

"We've got to go right back to the island and move that box of dynamite," Brent declared. "We don't want George and Clyde to get it if they go back there."

Kevin's round blue eyes looked scared. "Gee — I don't know," he said uneasily.

"Why did they hide it on the island, anyway?" Barbara asked. "What are they going to do with it?"

The boys glanced at each other.

"They could blow up one of the old buildings, just to scare Mr. Lindsay," Kevin said. "It might be part of their plan for driving him away."

Lucille stared. "Blow up one of the buildings? Ooh — what if they blew up the *barn*!"

She ran to get her bicycle. "We've got to go back and throw that dynamite into the creek or somewhere, quick! We don't want Pedro to be killed."

Trapped

THE SETTING SUN came out through a rift in the clouds just as they turned into the island lane. Its long, low rays touched the marsh grass, changing it from brown to dark red, and almost to purple. The light glinted in the creeks and flashed back from the windows of the old Moody house, too.

"It's beautiful, but it makes the island look more lonely than ever," Barbara sighed.

Lucille frowned. "I wish we didn't always get here just when it's growing dark."

"It won't take long to move the dynamite, but we've got to feed Pedro, too," Kevin reminded them.

They ignored the donkey's loud, eager greetings from the barn and hurried around to the carriage shed. The dynamite was still in the wagon.

"Ooh — be careful!" Lucille breathed, as the boys started to lift the box.

When they had it safely out of the wagon Brent suggested putting it in the henhouse. "Clyde and George will never look for it there. Boy, won't they be mad when they find out it's gone!"

The girls ran ahead to open the henhouse door. They moved some broken egg crates and a roll of chicken wire out of the way so the boys could set the dynamite in the farthest corner. Then they piled the things in front to hide it.

Lucille gave a huge sigh of relief. "Thank goodness that's done. The henhouse is so far from the barn nothing will happen to Pedro, even if the dynamite explodes."

"It won't," Kevin assured her again. "Not unless somebody makes it."

He gave her the key to the house and Brent handed the water pail to Barbara. "You can fill this while we give Pedro his oats."

Lucille sank onto a kitchen chair and let Barbara pump the water. "I'm bushed," she said. "I was so scared, while they were moving the dynamite, my knees just gave out." She reached around to where Mrs. Moody's cookbooks stood and took the scrapbook down from the shelf. "I wonder if there would be anything in here that would help — like a newspaper clipping of Mrs. Moody's marriage."

Kevin came in to get the water pail. "We're going to

let Pedro out for a few minutes," he said. "He needs exercise."

Barbara waved a limp hand. "Go ahead. We'll wait for you here."

"But hurry," Lucille urged, looking up from the scrapbook. "It's almost dark and we've got to get home."

Kevin grumbled at that. "Quarter past four isn't late."

Several minutes passed with hardly a sound but the ticking of the clock on the mantel. Both girls bent their heads over the yellowed clippings in the scrapbook, straining their eyes to read them.

Lucille pointed suddenly to a name at the end of a column called *Notes from Woods and Field.* "Hey — Mr. Lindsay wrote this!"

Yes, there was the name — Arnold Lindsay — signed to the clipping. The girls read it hastily. It was the story of a beaver dam that the beavers kept rebuilding when people tried to remove it from a small woods stream.

"Let's see if Mrs. Moody saved any other things he wrote," Barbara suggested eagerly.

They found many more copies of the column, all with Mr. Lindsay's name at the end.

"Now we know why she gave the island to him!" Barbara declared triumphantly. "He's a nature lover, and so was she. She knew he'd appreciate a place like this, with all the sea birds and marsh flowers and stuff."

Lucille's eyes sparkled with satisfaction. This proved that Mr. Lindsay was all right. There hadn't been anything underhanded in the way he got the island. She felt sure the dynamite wasn't his, either. Now if only they could find that wedding ring or something that would show Mrs. Moody really had been John Moody's wife, and really did own the island, *everything* would be all right.

She closed the book and stood up to put it back on the shelf. "The boys are taking their own sweet time," she muttered. "It's really dark. Let's go tell them to hurry up."

"I'm shivering all over now, instead of just in my knees," Barbara commented ruefully.

The house was cold. The chill had strengthened as the last rays of sun faded from the marsh outside the windows. A sudden sharp knock on the door made both girls step backward in fright. Barbara turned and reached for a heavy brass candlestick that stood on the mantel beside the clock. She held it behind her back while Lucille cautiously unlatched the door. "If it's those boys trying to scare us, I'll cl-clobber them," she stammered.

They were taken aback to see Miss Rand on the doorstep. She had a flat, square package tucked under one arm, and she looked as scared as the two girls felt.

"I hope I didn't frighten you," she said, peering into their alarmed faces. "I just wondered if anything was wrong down here."

She stepped into the kitchen without waiting to be asked. Crossing to the front room door, she disappeared in there for a second or two.

"Where are the boys?" she asked, when she returned — as if she had been looking for them. Lucille didn't notice that the package she had been carrying was gone.

"They're giving Pedro a chance to run around the yard. He's been shut in for two days," Barbara explained.

"I saw you children go down the lane quite a while ago," Miss Rand said. "I began to worry about you, and thought I'd better check and make sure you were all right. Luckily, Susan came to work early so I was able to duck out for a minute. I'll have to hurry back, now."

As soon as she was gone, Barbara returned the brass candlestick to the mantel. "You could kill a person with that, it's so heavy," she observed. "Maybe Mrs. Moody kept it here just for protection."

The boys came dashing in a few moments later. "What did Miss Rand want?" Kevin asked.

"That's a good question," Barbara replied. She gazed at Lucille thoughtfully. What had Miss Rand wanted — really?

A sound from the lane outside made all the children

fall silent. The planks of the bridge across the creek were rumbling. Somebody *else* was coming to the island!

Barbara ran to the window. "It's a car, and it hasn't got any lights. You can hardly see it."

They huddled together in the middle of the kitchen until they heard the car stop in the driveway. Then they tiptoed to the back window. They weren't at all surprised that it was George and Clyde who appeared in the dusk outside.

Kevin whispered to Lucille, "Give me the key. I'll lock the door so they can't get in here."

The young fellows hurried around the corner of the barn toward the carriage shed. What would they do when they discovered that the dynamite was gone?

"Thank goodness we hid it before they got here!" Lucille exclaimed.

Barbara was really frightened. She took hold of the doorknob and pleaded, "Let's go. We could get up to the street before they saw us."

But Clyde and George came striding back around the barn almost at once, talking in loud, angry tones. They rolled the barn door open and slipped inside. Instantly, Pedro's voice rang out, braying frightened *hee-haw's* that sounded like trumpet calls in the darkness. Both the intruders came stumbling out in a hurry.

"Good for Pedro," Brent muttered. "He's better than a watchdog."

George Turner looked toward the house, his gaze focusing on the window where the children were. They scrambled away from it, falling over each other in their fear of being seen. They tiptoed into the front room, and from there to the dark little hall. George wouldn't be able to see them there, even if he came right up to the house and peered in the windows.

They heard the kitchen doorknob rattle a few times. Then George muttered disgustedly, "Aw, let's go. The stuff wouldn't be in the house anyway." His grumbling voice receded as he and Clyde moved off to their car.

The four friends stole out of their hiding place and ran to the bay window in the front room, peering anxiously from the shadows on each side of it.

"If they put on their car lights they'll see our bikes!" Brent exclaimed in alarm.

Barbara gave a little gasp, and the others remembered with sinking hearts that they had left their bicycles lying on the grass close to the driveway. They hardly breathed while they waited for the car motor to start up. It sputtered a moment, then the car roared off with a rattle of gravel against screeching tires. But the lights did not go on.

With sighs of relief, the children ran to the kitchen, unlocked the door, and were back on their bicycles in less than a minute, headed straight for home. They were almost too tired to talk.

"We know — now — that it was George and Clyde

who put that dynamite in the carriage shed," Kevin said wearily. "We can prove it."

Brent sighed. "We can't do another thing until Mr. Lindsay gets home. Maybe, even then, Clyde will get the island."

Lucille thought of the lost wedding ring, and felt sad. Finding that was the one really helpful thing they could have done. But they had failed.

Last Minute Miracle

THE FOUR CHILDREN hurried back to the island the next afternoon without even stopping to eat. They saw Mr. Lindsay's car in the yard and ran to it eagerly. When they looked into it their faces fell. It was still piled high with suitcases and boxes.

"Maybe he isn't going to stay," Kevin sighed.

He called to them from the kitchen door. "Come in and get warm! I'm glad to see you again."

"Want us to help you unload your car?" Brent asked, before he even sat down.

Mr. Lindsay shook his head. "I don't know whether it's worthwhile to bother." He glanced at them questioningly. "I suppose you've heard the latest story Clyde's telling — about his uncle never having been married to the woman you knew as Mrs. Moody?"

They nodded. "But we don't believe it," Lucille assured him.

"Neither do I. I think it's Sam Estabrook who thought up that idea. He wants Clyde to have the island so he can buy it from him."

"You're not going to let them get away with it, are you?" Kevin asked.

Mr. Lindsay's voice sounded troubled. "I don't know. I might be able to fight that story — after all, it would be just as hard for Clyde to prove that his uncle and Margaret Moody were *not* married as for me to prove that they were. But I don't know." He shook his head. "It costs a lot of money to fight such a case in court. Maybe it's more than I can afford."

"We know why Mrs. Moody left the island to you," Lucille told him. She hopped up and got the old scrapbook. "She saved all your columns — *Notes from Woods and Field*. See?"

The little man glanced through the scrapbook in silence. When he finished, his voice was regretful. "I ought to put up a fight for *her* sake. She loved the marshes and the sea birds as much as I do."

He stood up and leaned against the kitchen table with his hands on his hips. He gazed at the children sternly. "Do *you* realize what it will mean if Clyde gets this island and sells it to Sam Estabrook?"

As they stared uneasily back at him he said, "Sam will fill in the marsh all the way from the island to the road. He will make another housing development out of it. That's what is happening to the marshes all up and down the Atlantic coast. They're being turned into marinas and house lots and even dumps."

He sounded so angry that Kevin asked, "Is that bad? I mean what harm does it do?"

"Our sea birds depend on the marshes for food and for resting places when they migrate. How would you like to make a turnpike trip from Maine to Florida and not find a single motel or restaurant along the way? Where would you eat? Or sleep? The marshes are the birds' motels and restaurants. Without them, they would die of hunger and weariness. And many of their marshes are drained or filled in already."

"Well, gee, we ought to try to save Nine-Mile. Every bit of it!" Kevin exclaimed.

He and Brent hastened to tell Mr. Lindsay about the dynamite they had found in the carriage shed. "We can prove it was Clyde and George who put it there. Wouldn't that help you?"

"Do you think they were planning to blow up the house, or the barn?" Barbara asked.

Mr. Lindsay smiled at them. "You children certainly proved yourselves to be my loyal friends, hiding that stuff and not telling anyone about it. I'm grateful to you." He removed his glasses, cleaned them on his handkerchief, and put them back on, while he thought for a minute. "I don't believe George and Clyde intended to blow up anything. I think it was all a part of their plan — and Estabrook's plan — to discredit me here in town. They will probably send the police over any minute to look for the dynamite and the painting."

The children looked bewildered. "The painting? What painting?"

Mr. Lindsay shrugged. "That was another unpleasant surprise I found when I got back here today. There was a package in the corner of the front hall. When I opened it I found a valuable painting — an original Brooks Waldron picture of a sunset over the marsh. I suppose George and Clyde took that from somewhere and put it here so I could be blamed for stealing it." He went into the front room and returned with a small, framed painting. Even in the fading light, it was so alive it seemed to glow.

Lucille clapped both hands over her mouth. Then she dropped them and exclaimed, "Oooh! Miss Rand!"

Mr. Lindsay looked at her in surprise. "What do you mean?"

"Miss Rand put the picture in your study! She came in here last night and went right to the front room. She had a flat package in her hands — "

"That's right!" Barbara cried. "She pretended she was looking for the boys. When she came back the package was gone. I remember it now, though I didn't notice it at the time."

"She's the one who would know about paintings, that's for sure," Kevin added.

Mr. Lindsay shrank back in his chair as if he wanted

to withdraw himself from what the children were saying. "Miss Rand is my friend. She has been very kind to me ever since we got acquainted. I can't believe she wants to drive me away. And I certainly don't believe she would steal anything."

"Then why did she put the painting here? And where did she get it?" Brent asked. "She *must* be trying to help Clyde and Mr. Estabrook."

Mr. Lindsay continued to shake his head. "It just wouldn't be like her. Brent, you and Kevin run up and tell her I need her help for a few minutes, will you? Tell her it's important."

The boys tore out of the house and up the lane on the run.

"It would be bad enough to lose the island," Mr. Lindsay said. "But I should feel much worse if I found I couldn't trust the people I've thought of as friends. I'm sure Miss Rand will be able to explain."

He got up and placed the painting on the mantel beside the clock, where the late sunshine from the window across the room lighted it up. Miss Rand's glance fell on it as soon as she stepped into the kitchen with the boys. She lowered her eyes and put one hand up to her flushed cheek. "Oh — was *that* what you wanted to see me about?"

Mr. Lindsay nodded. "I found it in my study. The girls remembered that you left a package there last night." He didn't ask any questions, but his blue eyes looked as if he expected some answers.

Miss Rand's voice, usually so firm, sounded low and miserable. "I stole it, you know. That's the plain truth."

"Stole it!" the children echoed.

Mr. Lindsay looked stunned. "But why did you leave it here? Were you trying to help Clyde and George get me into trouble? I — why, I can't believe it of you!"

"Get you in trouble?" Miss Rand's face looked startled. "How could it hurt you? It belongs here."

Everyone gasped at that. Mr. Lindsay slumped into a chair without a word. It was Lucille who finally broke the bewildered silence that had fallen upon the group.

"You stole the painting from *here!*" she exclaimed. "That's what you were trying to hide when we saw you sneaking up the lane the other day. That's how your blue handkerchief happened to be on the kitchen floor!"

Miss Rand nodded. "I didn't intend to steal it, but I *had* to find out if there really was an original Brooks Waldron painting in this house. I knew Waldron and John Moody had been friends, years ago. They used to go fishing together. Brooks Waldron gave sketches and paintings to a few other friends in this town and I got the idea he might have given one to old John. I tried to find out first by calling on Mrs. Moody, but she wouldn't even let me in the house."

She glanced apologetically at Mr. Lindsay. "When

I saw you go off for a walk that first afternoon I wondered if you might have left your doors unlocked. It seemed like my only chance to look for the painting. I didn't think you — or Clyde, either — deserved to have it, if it was there. I didn't know you then, of course. Anyway — I found it hanging in the dark little front hall where it could hardly be seen. That made me furious! You know how I feel about paintings. So I — well — I just took it." She bit her lip, and for a moment Lucille was afraid she was going to burst into tears.

"And I hadn't even noticed it," Mr. Lindsay said. He added gently, "You brought it back, though. Would you mind explaining why?"

Miss Rand's plump face turned red. "Well," she said, "when I got to know you I realized you were — I mean, I liked you. I felt as if we were friends. So I couldn't keep the painting. It belonged to you."

Mr. Lindsay began to smile. "*I* thought we were friends, too. I told the children you couldn't be trying to hurt me."

Lucille laughed softly and clasped her hands in secret pleasure. This was the way friends ought to be, and it made her feel good to see it.

"I just hope you can keep the painting," Kevin said to Mr. Lindsay. "If Clyde gets the island he'll get that, too, won't he?"

Miss Rand cried, "Oh no! You mustn't let him."

Mr. Lindsay got up restlessly and poked a stick of

wood into the stove. The flames lighted the dusky room for a minute. It seemed full of shadows when the lids were closed again.

"Golly, I forgot to fill my lamps," he said. "I'd better do that right away."

"There are some candles on the top shelf in the pantry," Lucille said.

She got one and reached for the heavy brass candlestick on the mantel to put it in. The candle didn't seem to fit, so she pulled a bobby pin from her hair and poked into the hole. "This thing is full of wax," she muttered.

One big lump came out into her hand, but there still wasn't room for the candle. She turned the candlestick upside down and dug at it again.

Something tiny and glittering suddenly dropped onto the floor with a metallic clink. Brent and Kevin bumped their heads together as they scrambled after it. Lucille lighted the candle and held it down so they could see.

Kevin came up first, triumphantly holding out a small circlet of gold. "It's the — " he drew in his breath in his usual gasp of excitement — "It's the ring!"

The children stumbled over each other as they tried to tell the story of the lost wedding ring to the two grown-ups.

Mr. Lindsay took it and held it carefully in the candlelight. "J. M. to M. B. April 1936," he read in a solemn voice. "John Moody to Margaret Somebody-or-other. So they *were* married! This ring is real proof of it!"

"Do you think it is proof that will stand up in court?" Miss Rand asked anxiously.

Mr. Lindsay turned to Lucille. "You say the diary tells about the lost ring in Mrs. Moody's own handwriting?"

"Oh, yes!"

"Well, then I'm sure the two things together will be proof enough to satisfy any judge. I don't think Sam Estabrook and Clyde will even bother to take it to court when they learn about this."

He placed it on the table in the circle of candlelight and they all stared in still-amazed silence at the small gold band.

"Hee-haw!"

The loud bray, from somewhere just outside, made them all jump. "Good heavens, I forgot about Pedro," Mr. Lindsay cried. He opened the door. The donkey's big head and tall gray ears appeared in the opening. Pedro had got tired of waiting for his friends to come and play with him.

"Come right in. Yessir, right into this kitchen!" Mr. Lindsay said, putting his arm around Pedro's neck. "Who's got a better right? Why, without you I might never have met these children, and never have found the ring. You and I might have lost our island."

Miss Rand laughed. "I suppose we do have him to thank for this last-minute miracle."

Finding the ring really had been a miracle, Lucille thought, as she gazed happily at the blinking donkey. His hoofs, that were still a bit clumsy, stumbled on the doorsill. Everyone petted him, and Mr. Lindsay fed him a handful of cookies. And only two weeks ago he had been tied out in that old cabbage garden in the rain! Thank goodness he was safe, at last.

Mr. Lindsay smiled at Miss Rand. "About the painting. You appreciate it much more than I do. We must find some way to share it. I'd like to reward these children, too. Could I put in an order for sodas and hot dogs for them at The Blue Goose — free — whenever they want them?"

Miss Rand laughed. "Certainly you could. Only — if you and I are to share the painting — you must let *me* foot the bill for the free snacks. It would give me a way of making up for stealing the picture. I still feel guilty about that."

"Oh, boy! Oh, brother! Hot dogs and Cokes — unlimited!" Kevin and Brent exclaimed together.

Barbara gazed around the small, candlelit room in confusion. "Everything happened too fast," she protested. "We found out about everything all at once!"

Kevin's voice was suddenly thoughtful. "Not everything," he reminded her. "We didn't find out about the Moody noises. We still don't know about them."

Lucille's eyes happened to rest on Mr. Lindsay's

face at that moment. She was surprised at the uneasy, almost guilty look that came over it. He knew! He had found out what caused the noises. She felt almost sure of it.

Miss Rand shook her head at Kevin. "I hope nobody ever finds out about them. They make this island seem romantic and ghostly. They're good for my business, you know."

Mr. Lindsay looked squarely at the children. "You don't want to do away with all the mystery, do you?"

They hesitated.

"Do you mean you think it's more fun *not* to know about the noises?" Barbara asked.

He nodded. "What other place do you know of that has its own real live ghost? A screeching, wailing ghost that *anyone* can hear? Moody's Island would be pretty tame without it. If I knew — I mean, if I ever found out — what made the Moody noises, I'd carry the secret to my grave."

Lucille whispered to Barbara, "I think he knows already. I wish he'd tell us."

Barbara smiled at her teasingly. "You're the one who said it was more fun to do things by ourselves. We've already had heaps of fun that way."

Lucille glanced through the window in a dreamy silence. She could see the darkened marshes stretching toward the sea with the last of the sunset light lingering on them. Would it be better to leave the mysterious noises unexplained forever? Then Nine-Mile

Marsh would always be haunted by something as strangely out-of-this-world as the glow in the Brooks Waldron painting.

Kevin grinned at Brent and declared firmly, "It's going to be great fun to keep trying to find out about the noises, and to ride Pedro, and to have free snacks at The Blue Goose. But no matter what we do, we'll never have a better time than we've had this afternoon, right here in this little old kitchen."

And the smiles that brightened the faces of the others seemed to show that they all agreed with him.